Oscar hates his life, but he's too frightened to do anything about it. The last time he did the right thing — when he freed James, the bitten werewolf accused of killing the pack's alpha — his father whipped him, and he's still recovering from that. He knows he won't be able to go through that again, but when one of the conclave enforcers comes back to ask a few more questions after they arrest James, he knows he can't keep the truth to himself, no matter how fearful he is of the consequences.

Ignatius wasn't sure his friend Fyfe was right when he called and asked him to make sure James really was guilty of murder, but now that he's been back with the pack interrogating witnesses again, he knows something is wrong. He gets the proof he needs when Oscar, the new alpha's son, tells him his father is behind everything. Ignatius is alone, though, so there's not much he can do. Alpha Becket won't let Oscar go, but Ignatius won't leave him behind.

He'll never forgive himself if he does, conclave rules be damned.

Perfect Fangs
Copyright © 2019 Catherine Lievens
ISBN: 978-1-4874-2603-3
Cover art by Angela Waters

Published by eXtasy Books Inc or
Devine Destinies, an imprint of eXtasy Books Inc

Look for us online at:
www.eXtasybooks.com or www.devinedestinies.com

PERFECT FANGS
LIFE WITH FANGS BOOK 3

BY

CATHERINE LIEVENS

CHAPTER ONE

Oscar reached out to grab the bottle of water on his nightstand and grimaced when the movement pulled on the wounds that were still healing on his back. This was the first time his father had ever whipped him, and he hoped it would be the last time.

He was no stranger to bruises and blood. His father wasn't a good man, and people — including Oscar — didn't respect him. That meant his father had to use force for most people to obey him, and Oscar's disobedience had been humiliating for him, so much so that for once, he'd ignored his own rule not to hurt people so much they couldn't move.

Oscar didn't regret it, though. He couldn't, not when he knew what would have happened to James if he hadn't freed him. He *did* regret not going with James, but he'd thought this would be safer for both of them. And maybe he was right. He had no idea what had happened to James since he'd left, and while Oscar was in pain, he was alive. His father would never kill him, not when he could be useful to him.

And he would be, as soon as he could move normally. His father had already told him about the deal he'd made with a nearby pack. They wanted a born werewolf, and he'd sold Oscar to them. He'd probably end up married to the alpha's daughter or someone equally important, and he'd have to give her werewolf babies.

He snorted. *Good luck with that.* He wasn't even sure his dick would get hard for a woman, and that wasn't counting the fact that he'd be a prisoner, married to a woman he didn't know, in a place he didn't know, no doubt guarded so he couldn't escape.

He opened the bottle and took a sip, grimacing when that movement, too, pulled on his wounds. There wasn't much that didn't, so he tried to spend most of his time on his bed, stretched out on his stomach. He wasn't allowed to leave his room anyway, so it wasn't that hard, but he could have killed for a painkiller. Well, not killed, but snuck downstairs to grab one. He would have if he hadn't been afraid to be discovered because he was moving slowly. His bedroom door wasn't locked, because his father *wanted* him to disobey so he'd have a reason to punish him again.

Oscar wasn't going to do that. He'd had enough with one whipping, thank you very much.

The sound of tires on the gravel made him look up. He'd had to sit to be able to drink, so it wasn't much harder to haul himself off the bed to go peek out the window. Every movement stung, but he pushed through, gritting his teeth. Finding out who was there was vital. Oscar needed to know, because if something was going to happen to him, he had to be prepared.

He leaned his hand against the window frame and took a deep breath. His legs felt like jelly, and he needed the support.

He pushed the curtain to the side and frowned. He didn't know the bike, and he knew what everyone in the pack drove. Was it someone from the pack where he'd be sent when he felt better and when his father was more secure in his new alpha position? Maybe they'd had enough of waiting. Maybe they wanted Oscar to start making werewolf pups as soon as possible. Oscar wouldn't be surprised. A lot of people thought that the only good werewolf was a born one, which was stupid, but then a lot of people *were* stupid.

The bike stopped, and Oscar moved closer to the window to get a better look. It took him a moment to recognize the man that took his helmet off, because he'd been in his room most of the time since he'd helped James escape, and his father had made sure that the only things he told the conclave enforcers were the ones he'd approved. Oscar wasn't sure what he'd told them—probably that James had managed to get out of his cell alone—but Oscar was sure he hadn't mentioned him, because the enforcers would have wanted to talk to him then.

His father couldn't have allowed it, because he'd whipped him to the point where he could barely move, and he'd used the excuse that Oscar was sick and that he hadn't seen anything to make sure they didn't get close to him. Whipping pack members wasn't forbidden, of course, but it showed he was angrier than warranted. Even if the enforcers believed James had killed Alpha Torres and that Oscar's father had been angry that he was set free, who would whip their own son for that?

Oscar's father was angry, yes, but he was also terrified because *he* was the one who'd killed Alpha Torres, not James, and he needed that to stay a secret.

Oscar opened the window once the conclave man was out of sight on the porch. He leaned closer, and he heard the knock on the door and the door opening.

"What do you want?" his father snapped. Then, in a more normal voice, he asked, "Did you find the man who killed my alpha? Did you find James?"

Oscar's stomach churned. He *hated* his father. He was pretty sure everyone in the pack hated him, even though they didn't know he was the one who'd killed their alpha. Alpha Torres had been a good man. The fact that he'd decided to help a bitten werewolf had created some controversy, especially when James hadn't magically managed to control his wolf right off the bat. But Alpha Torres had been the alpha, and everyone had followed his orders. He'd always made sure the pack was safe and that all its members had a home and food to eat.

Oscar wouldn't be surprised if that changed now that his father was in charge.

"We did." The enforcer's voice was rumbly and made Oscar's stomach feel weird.

"What are you doing here, then? You have the killer."

"My team leader sent me to make sure we have all the information and details we need."

"He killed Torres. What more do you need to know?"

"The conclave takes its job very seriously, Alpha Becket. We thoroughly investigate all the situations we're called into, and that includes this one. The rest of my team is interrogating the werewolf right now, and they will no doubt get the answers we need, but we also need confirmation on a few things, and that's where I come in. I'd like to talk to the witnesses again and make sure there are no inconsistencies to their stories, as well as talking to your son, since he wasn't interrogated the first time we were here. I realize all the physical proof is gone, but I'm going to go over what happened, follow in James' footsteps, and make sure everything is as it's supposed to be." He paused. "Although of course, I'm still on the porch."

Oscar could imagine his father's reaction. His eyes were probably narrowed as he tried to find a way to get out of this and couldn't. Oscar imagined the enforcer couldn't care less about what his father wanted, and that fact gave him a thrill. The pack needed someone who didn't care, although he realized that the enforcer wasn't going to be staying. He'd investigate, find what he needed, and leave, and the pack would be back at square one, with a terrible, cruel alpha that no one deserved.

"Of course. Come in," Oscar's father finally said. "The pack will help you in any way we can. Our loss was a terrible one, and James needs to pay for what he did."

Oscar closed the window and rushed to the door. He held his breath as he opened it. He didn't want to sneak downstairs and risk being caught by his father, but he wanted to know about this enforcer and what was going to happen in the next few days. Maybe Oscar could somehow make him realize what was happening. He couldn't come out and say it, not outright, not if he didn't want to be whipped again, but he had to find a way.

James shouldn't pay for something he hadn't done. Oscar wasn't going to allow that, and if the enforcer couldn't find a way to prove James was innocent, Oscar was going to have to step in. It was terrifying, but it was right, and Oscar would never forgive himself if James was executed for something his father had done. He'd stayed quiet even though he'd known his father was planning something, and Alpha Torres had died.

He wasn't going to stay quiet this time. He couldn't.

Ignatius knew the alpha was hiding something. It would have been obvious to him even if he didn't have the training he had. This man didn't want him anywhere near his house or his pack, and now Ignatius was convinced more than ever that something wasn't right.

Damn it. Fyfe was right to push. He'd seen something neither Ignatius nor the other people in his team had seen, and Ignatius hated that.

He'd become a conclave enforcer because he'd wanted to do something with his never-ending life. He wanted to keep the world safe from the monsters that lurked in the night, from the paranormal entities who killed people because they thought it was their right. But that wasn't the case with James, yet Ignatius had let what he knew about the man cloud his judgment, and he'd ignored all the tiny details that just didn't fit with Alpha Becket's narration.

Ignatius wasn't going to let an innocent pay for something someone else had done. It had nothing to do with the fact that from the sound of it, Fyfe knew exactly where James was and was probably half in love with him.

He followed Alpha Becket to his office. He'd been in Alpha Torres' office the first time he and the team had been around, and this office was nothing like that. Alpha Torres had been all for comfort and putting the people who came to him at ease, and he'd filled his office with comfortable chairs and couches.

This office was an ode to Alpha Becket. There were trophies everywhere, and pictures of Becket with dead animals he'd apparently hunted. Ignatius knew the alpha had a son, yet there were no signs of him in the room. The fact that Becket didn't seem to care much for the kid didn't mean much, but it was one more thing that made Ignatius wary of him.

"Sit," Becket ordered.

Ignatius knew which battles to fight and which to ignore, so he sat, but the rudeness was another strike against the alpha. Ignatius wasn't just a vampire. He was a conclave enforcer, and Becket knew better than to treat him like that didn't mean anything.

"What do you want, exactly?" Alpha Becket asked.

"I'd like to talk to the people who gave us the information the last time we were here again."

"You already talked to them."

"I'm aware of that. But now that we have James, we'll get more information from him, and we need to make sure everything fits together."

Becket glared. "Are you accusing me of lying?"

"No. But memories are tricky things, and the conclave can't

afford to act unless we're a hundred percent sure of what we're doing. We'd lose the respect we built up over hundreds of years if we executed a man without being entirely sure he's guilty."

"He *is* guilty. I told you that. He killed Alpha Torres."

"Then I don't see why me talking to the witnesses again should be a problem."

There was no way out of this for Becket, and from the look on his face, he knew it. "It's not, of course. I just wanted to avoid useless work for you."

"It's not useless, and it's what I'm paid to do. Do I have free rein, then?"

"I wouldn't want you to get lost in pack territory. It would be better if I put a guard with you."

"I don't need a guard. I'll be just fine on my own, but thank you."

"But—"

"And of course, if you have any problems with my presence here or the reason I'm here, feel free to contact my superior. You've already met him, and I know Oren left you his phone number. You can leave a complaint with him, and he'll make sure I'm investigated. Of course, that would no doubt bring more attention to your pack on the conclave's part, but I don't think that would be a problem, would it?"

"Of course not. We have nothing to hide."

But Becket did. It was as plain as the nose on his face, at least to Ignatius. He could see it in the way Becket kept pressing his lips together, in the way he crossed and uncrossed his arms over his chest repeatedly, in the way he cleared his throat too often to be normal, unless he had a cold and his throat hurt.

Becket cleared his throat again. "Who are you going to talk to first?" he asked.

"I have a list of witnesses. I'll go through it and keep you informed on what's happening."

"I could go with you, just to put my people at ease while you interrogate them."

That was a rather desperate attempt. "No, thank you. I want them to feel like they can freely talk to me, and while I'm sure they'd be comfortable with you there, I don't want to risk it."

"I wouldn't try to influence them."

"I never said you would. But people tend to want to please their alphas. I've seen it happen often enough over the years. And of course, we enforcers work alone, or with other enforcers. Thank you for proposing to help me, but you should stay here." Ignatius got up, and Becket scrambled to follow him.

Ignatius resisted the urge to smile. "I'm sure you're very busy. All alphas are. I can find the way out on my own, thank you." He frowned. "Oh, and I'll need to talk to your son." Becket's son was one of the witnesses Ignatius' team had talked to. Ignatius hadn't been the one to do it, though, so he wasn't sure what to expect from the man.

Becket cleared his throat. "He's asleep right now. He hasn't been feeling well."

"It can wait. Like I said, I have a list." He nodded. "Thank you for your help. I can find the way out on my own."

Ignatius left the office before Becket could try to find another reason for him not to wander in pack territory alone. He didn't know Becket well, but he'd met plenty of men like him over the hundreds of years since he'd become a vampire. The man wasn't going to be a good alpha, and he knew it. He was the kind of man who used their power over their people to abuse them, the kind of man who always wanted more—power, money, and respect they earned through violence.

There definitely was something odd going on, and Ignatius wouldn't leave until he found out what it was. He wouldn't be able to do anything, not on his own, and especially because he wasn't there on conclave business, but he could go back to Oren with the new information and make sure Oren knew who was behind Alpha Torres' murder. Oren could contact the conclave and have them decide what they wanted to do. The fact that Becket was an alpha wouldn't change the way they'd deal with him if he'd been the one behind Alpha Torres' death. The conclave and its enforcers didn't care what a person was. They meted out justice, and that was what they'd do this time, too.

Ignatius left the house and went back to his bike. He'd left the list with the names and the information on the people he needed to talk to in his backpack. He leaned against his seat as he gave it a quick read through, trying to decide who he was going to talk to first.

When he looked up, he noticed a curtain moving on the second floor of the house. He didn't look right at it. Instead, he faked interest in his documents, but he could see well enough from where he was—a blond man was peeking through the window, looking at him. He was half-hidden by the curtain, but visible enough that Ignatius could see he was painfully young.

He went back to his notes to find the ones on Oscar, Becket's son. He was twenty-four years old, but he looked younger from the little Ignatius had seen. Ignatius was curious to find out if he was like his father, or if there was more to him. He'd suspected Oscar wasn't asleep, and he was right. That meant Becket didn't want him to talk to his son, and *that* meant that Oscar knew something about what had happened to James, and possibly about Alpha Torres' death.

And Ignatius was going to find out what that was.

Oscar jerked back when the enforcer looked straight at his window. Pain flared in his back, and he bit on his lower lip.

He didn't want his father to hear him crying out. That wouldn't end well for him. His interactions with his father never did.

That was why he also couldn't allow his father to find out he'd caught the enforcer's attention. He hadn't meant to do it, but he'd heard why the enforcer was there, and he'd been curious.

The fact that the man was like a walking wet dream might also have influenced Oscar, of course. The enforcer was tall, with dark hair that curled around his ears and on his forehead. Oscar wanted to tug on those curls and see what happened, although he doubted that he'd be able to move much even if he got that close to the man. His back was killing him, which meant he should probably go stretch out on his bed again to rest. He'd heard that the enforcer wanted to talk to him, and he expected his father to come to his bedroom soon to warn him about what he'd do to him if he said anything he shouldn't.

Oscar didn't need the warning. His back hurt more than enough for him to know what would happen to him if he said something he shouldn't.

He'd just lain back on his bed when his bedroom door slammed open. He jumped, grimacing at the pain in his back, and sat on the edge of the mattress. "Father?"

"You know about the enforcer?"

Oscar's father had been too busy with the enforcer to make sure Oscar wasn't listening, and Oscar hoped he could use that to his advantage. "What enforcer, Father?"

"The one who was just here."

"I'm sorry. I was asleep. I didn't sleep well—"

"I don't care how you slept." Oscar's father paced the length of the bedroom. "An enforcer just came. He wants to talk to you and the other people who witnessed what happened with James and Alpha Torres."

Oscar's chest felt tight with hope and fear. "I understand."

His father stopped in front of him and grabbed the collar of his shirt. He pulled him up, and Oscar dug his nails into the palms of his hands. He *couldn't* cry out and give his father an indication of the pain he was in.

His father gave him a shake. "You're not going to tell him anything."

"I won't. I promise."

"If you do, I'll whip you again, and I won't hold back this time."

Hold back? Oscar wasn't sure how he'd survived the first whipping, but he knew he couldn't go through another one. He wasn't strong enough. "I won't say anything," he repeated, praying his father would believe him.

In truth, he didn't know what he'd do. He'd let James go because he didn't want an innocent to pay for what his father had done, and he still didn't want that to happen. James was his friend, the only person who'd braved his father's ire and had become close to him. He didn't want James to be hurt, or worse, but what his father was saying meant he might have to choose between his own safety and James, and he had no idea how to do that.

Oscar didn't have anyone, not now that James was gone. He didn't have anyone to protect him if he told the truth. He couldn't even be sure the conclave would do something about his father, because he had no proof that he was the one behind Alpha Torres' death, not beyond his word. Would that be enough for the conclave, or would they abandon him to his father's ire?

Oscar wasn't sure he could risk it. Maybe after he talked to the enforcer, if he managed to get an idea of what the man thought and of what he might do if he talked. But not before.

Oscar's father let him go, and Oscar dropped back on the bed. His back was on fire, but he couldn't dwell on that, because his father backhanded him. He slammed into the wall by the bed, and now his entire body was in pain—his back, his face, and his arm and side where he'd hit the wall.

His father shook his hand. "I shouldn't have done that, but you always push me, Oscar."

Oscar hadn't said anything that would have warranted that, but then, he never did. His father was an asshole. Nothing Oscar did or said would change that fact or his actions, and Oscar had gotten used to that idea long ago.

Sometimes he wondered if his father had always been this way. He couldn't remember a time when he hadn't been, but maybe when his mother was still alive? She'd been killed by a bitten wolf when Oscar was four, and since then, he'd only had his father. Was that where his father's hatred of bitten wolves came? Probably, but Oscar didn't understand why the hatred hadn't touched him. His father had lost his wife, but *he'd* lost his mother. Shouldn't he hate bitten wolves as much as his father did? That was one of the reasons his father had killed Alpha Torres. It didn't excuse anything, and Oscar was past feeling sorry for what had happened and for his father's loss. He'd lost just as much, yet he'd never targeted his hatred on people who hadn't done anything to deserve it. James might be a bitten wolf, but he hadn't chosen that, and he had no way to change it.

Oscar's father could have changed if he wanted to. He could have not killed their alpha, and he could have tried to be a better man instead of letting pain turn into hate.

Oscar wasn't sure what he'd do, but his father deserved to pay, and he was going to make that happen.

"You'll keep your mouth shut," his father said. "I told him you weren't feeling well, so act like it."

That wasn't going to be a problem. "I will."

Oscar stayed right where he was until his father left, slamming the door behind him. He still didn't lock it, and Oscar wished he was stronger, that he'd dare to shift and run away.

But he didn't.

He didn't have anyone outside the pack. Hell, he didn't have anyone inside the pack. The only person who'd ever been friends with him was James, and Oscar had no way to find out where he was or if he was safe. He couldn't go to him, not when it looked like the enforcers had caught him or were at least close to catching him.

Oscar pushed himself up from the bed and went to the small bathroom that was attached to his bedroom. The light in there was harsh and hurt his eyes, but he leaned close to the mirror to check on what his father had done to him.

There would be a bruise on his cheek. That much was obvious. There was no way the enforcer wouldn't notice, but then, people always noticed when Oscar's father beat him, and no one ever did anything to help him. It wasn't their business, their problem, and Oscar understood. The only people who saw were pack embers, and there was little they could do to help.

Would the enforcer try, though? Oscar wanted to hope, but he'd given up on hope a long time ago. He couldn't count on hope to survive. He could only count on himself for that.

He wanted support, though. He'd yearned for it all his life, and he'd found it in James. Maybe if he managed to get to him, but how was he supposed to do that?

Oscar sighed and brushed his fingertips against the skin that was already started to swell. It was a pointless dream, wasn't it? How was he supposed to leave this place when he didn't even know where to go? What would happen if he decided to shift and just run? He'd have to stop sooner or later, and when he did, he wouldn't have money, a phone, or even clothes. He'd be just as alone as he was now, just as unable to do anything.

But there was one thing he could do. He could tell the

enforcer what had happened, once he was sure he could trust the man to do something about it and not to report back to his father. Then he'd only have hope left—hope that the conclave would try to stop his father rather than look the other way, hope that he'd be freed eventually and that he'd manage to do something with his life.

No matter how useless it was, hope was *all* he had.

This was frustrating.

Ignatius had talked to one of the witnesses, and he'd gotten the same thing they'd told the rest of his team the first time around—word for word. That alone would have made it obvious the man was lying, but the fact that he also kept looking at his front door, bouncing his knee, and that he'd been sweating as if his house were an oven, had reinforced Ignatius' opinion that something was going on here.

And he had a pretty good idea of what that something was.

He went over the notes he'd taken one last time. The man, Roger, had found Alpha Torres dead in his backyard. He'd come to the alpha's house to talk to him about his job, and he'd arrived from the back, in his wolf form. He'd freaked out when he'd seen his alpha dead, but especially at the claw marks that had made the way he'd died evident.

And that was where Ignatius got stuck. Alpha Torres had been killed by a werewolf in their wolf form. There was no disputing that. But how did anyone know James had been that shifter? He was just one wolf in a pack of wolves, and while it was true that he'd only been recently bitten and that he didn't have control over his wolf, that didn't mean he was the killer. There was no proof of that, and it looked more and more like the pack, or rather, their new alpha, had decided that James was the killer just because he wanted an easy scapegoat. Whether that was because he didn't want to investigate or because he already knew who the killer was, though, Ignatius had no idea.

He needed to talk to the other witnesses, but he suspected the answers he'd get would be the same as the ones he already had, and that wasn't going to help him find out what had happened. He suspected he already knew, but he needed proof. The conclave didn't go around arresting people because they thought a crime had been committed.

That thought made Ignatius' stomach churn. That was what they were doing with James, wasn't it? They'd been told James had killed Alpha Torres and that he was a dangerous, uncontrollable bitten wolf, and they'd rushed to find him. They *did* need to find him, if anything because they needed to hear his version of this, but Ignatius could admit they weren't doing this the right way.

He put his notebook away and rubbed his face. Since when did he and his team behave like this? He didn't like the thought, and while he knew Oren was a good man and a great team leader, he couldn't deny they'd almost botched this investigation. He needed to get it right and make sure James didn't pay for something he hadn't done, though.

He made his way back to the alpha's house. The forest was dark, and he doubted he'd find any of the other witnesses awake. Being a vampire and not being able to go in the sun without burning was tricky sometimes, which was why the conclave teams had members that belonged to several races of paranormal beings. But Ignatius was on his own this time, and he'd have to deal with that.

The light was still on in the room where he'd seen the curtain move earlier. Maybe he *could* talk to another witness tonight. He was sure Alpha Becket would have something to say about that, but Ignatius didn't care. He was there to do his job, and he knew the pack was hiding something and protecting their new alpha. From what he knew of Becket, they were probably doing it out of fear rather than because they liked him.

He climbed the porch steps and knocked on the front door. He could smell food, so he wasn't surprised when the alpha opened the door still cleaning his mouth with a napkin. "What are you doing here?" Becket asked.

"I wanted to talk to your son."

"He's asleep."

"The light is on in his bedroom." And since Becket was eating, why wasn't his son having dinner with him? Was he really not feeling well, or was Becket trying to delay Ignatius' chat with him? "And I'm sure he'd like some dinner."

Becket glared. "I was going to bring him up a tray."

"Of course. Then I can probably talk to him while he's eating. I promise I'll leave as soon as he's done so he can get some rest."

Ignatius watched as the alpha no doubt tried to find a reason for him not to enter. He could insist his son wasn't feeling well, but like Ignatius had pointed out, the boy needed to eat, and Ignatius needed to talk to him before he could declare the investigation over.

Becket nodded. "All right. I'm going to get him a tray. Stay here," he said, stepping to the side to let Ignatius in.

Ignatius obeyed. He had no intention of seeing more of the house than he had to. He didn't usually go around interrogating people in their bedroom, but he couldn't avoid it this time, not when Becket insisted his son was ill. Ignatius still wasn't sure that was the case, but he was about to find out.

Becket came back with a tray in his hands. It held a small bottle of water and a plate containing what looked like part of a well-done steak. There were no vegetables, no sauces, and Ignatius didn't envy Oscar his dinner. Ignatius might be on a liquid blood diet, but it was more appetizing than the steak.

Becket grunted and went up the stairs, Ignatius right

behind him. The house was oddly decorated, with pieces of furniture that looked like they didn't belong together, all covered with a layer of dust that should make any werewolf sneeze. Becket didn't knock when he got to his son's bedroom. He barged into the room as if it was his right, and while it might be since he was the boy's father, the owner of the house, and the pack's alpha, it left a bitter taste in Ignatius' mouth. He didn't like disrespectful people and people who used their position to terrorize people, and it was obvious that Oscar was afraid of his father from the moment Ignatius stepped into the room.

Oscar was huddled on his bed, and his brown eyes went wide when he saw Ignatius. Ignatius knew Oscar was twenty-four, yet he looked younger, all blond hair and big eyes — and fear. Ignatius could smell it even though he wasn't a werewolf.

Becket dumped the tray onto the desk in the corner of the room and crossed his arms over his chest. "There. You can ask him all the questions you need."

Ignatius forced himself to smile. "I will, thank you. But I need to talk to him alone."

"Why? That's not going to change what he has to say."

Ignatius doubted that. "Maybe not, but it's conclave policy to interrogate witnesses alone. I'll let you know when I'm done and leaving. Thank you for allowing me into your home."

Becket had no choice but to leave, not unless he wanted Ignatius to realize something was going on. Of course, Ignatius already had. He'd be a poor investigator if he hadn't.

Becket grunted. "Fine. Oscar, behave. Got it?"

Oscar nodded, his hair flopping on his forehead. "Of course, Father." His voice trembled just a bit, and Ignatius didn't miss the way he leaned back when his father walked past the bed on his way out.

Becket slammed the door shut, but Ignatius kept his gaze on Oscar, who relaxed as soon as the door was closed behind his father. Yes, there was fear there, and when Oscar moved and hissed in discomfort, Ignatius knew there was also violence and abuse.

Nothing made him angrier than when alphas or coven leaders used their position to hurt people, especially when those people were someone they were supposed to love and cherish, like children. Oscar was twenty-four, but that didn't mean he wasn't vulnerable.

"Hello, Oscar," he said, trying not to scare Oscar.

Oscar swallowed, his throat bobbing. "Hello."

"Can I sit next to you?"

Oscar eyed the bed. "There's a chair at the desk."

"I know. I'd like to sit next to you, though. Please." He needed to, but he wasn't going to spook Oscar.

Oscar finally nodded, and Ignatius settled on the edge of the mattress, close enough that when he extended his arm, the tip of his fingers touched Oscar's foot. Oscar sucked in a breath, but he didn't move, and he stared at Ignatius with wide eyes—eyes Ignatius knew it would be easy to lose himself in.

CHAPTER TWO

Oscar didn't move. He wasn't sure why, because people didn't just touch him the way this man was. The only person who did was his father, and that was when he hit him. But Oscar could tell the enforcer wouldn't hurt him. He had kind eyes.

"My name is Ignatius."

Oscar cleared his throat. "Oscar. But you probably already know that."

Ignatius smiled. "You're right, I do. The reason I'm touching you right now is that I have the power to cloak us. No one will be able to hear what we're talking about as long as I keep touching you. That means that even if your father is right outside this door with his ear pressed against it, he won't hear what you're telling me. I can stop touching you if you're uncomfortable, but I was hoping that knowing this would help you relax. You can tell me the truth."

Oscar wasn't sure what to do with that. He hadn't decided what he'd do yet, what he'd tell this enforcer, and the fact that his father couldn't hear him helped only in part. He wouldn't be able to stop him if he decided to speak the truth, but Oscar still didn't know what would happen to him if he did.

"Do you—do you really have James?" he asked instead of telling Ignatius what he wanted to hear.

"He's safe. Don't worry."

"He left this place because he was being hunted by you and your team."

Ignatius sighed. "You're right. We made a mistake, and I'm

not proud of it. We should have dug deeper than we did. But I am now, and I intend to find out exactly what happened. I need help, though. I've already talked to one of the witnesses, Roger, and he repeated what he already told us the first time we talked to him. He found Alpha Torres' body. The alpha bore claw marks on his body, and Roger thinks it was James. He didn't tell me *why* he thinks that, though, and as far as I can see, no one can. There's no proof James killed anyone."

"My father says it has to be him because he's a bitten wolf. He can't control his wolf yet."

"Yet you freed James, didn't you?"

Oscar licked his lips. "Who told you that? James?"

"No. I'm just guessing, but you seem to care for James, while everyone else is too afraid of your father to do something like that. I can't imagine he reacted well when he found the cell empty."

Oscar shivered at the memory. "He didn't."

"Will you tell me what happened, then?"

Oscar wanted to. He wanted James to be free and safe. He also wanted *himself* to be free and safe, though, and he had no guarantee that would happen.

What if he told Ignatius what his father had done, and Ignatius decided to leave him in place as the alpha anyway? The conclave didn't intervene when it came to alphas' succession, although they should arrest Oscar's father. They might not want to, though, because who would take his place at the head of the pack? Oscar certainly wouldn't. He never wanted to see this place again once—or rather, if—he managed to get away.

But if the conclave left his father alone, he'd make sure Oscar could never talk about what he'd done again.

"We'll protect you, if that's what you're afraid of," Ignatius said.

"You were going to let James pay for a murder he didn't

commit. You hunted him without even talking to him first. You believed my father when he told you James had been the one who'd killed Alpha Torres."

Ignatius grimaced. "You're right. We fucked up. I know that, and I suspect my team leader does, too. But we do have to talk to James, and running the way he did made him look guilty."

"But he *wasn't* guilty."

"And you know that for sure."

Oscar bit his lower lip. He was going to have to do this, wasn't he? He couldn't let James pay for what his father had done, and even though he didn't know what would happen to him or to his father once he spoke the truth, he knew he could leave the pack. He had nowhere to go, no friends, but anything would be better than staying with the pack even if he had to live in his wolf form in the forest for the foreseeable future.

"Can you promise me you'll make sure James doesn't pay if I tell you the truth?" he asked.

"I can. I made a mistake — *we* made a mistake. But we're not going to repeat it. The conclave was created to make sure that justice was present in a world where some of us live forever, where it was too easy for us to do what we wanted just because no one was there to make us face the consequences of our actions. That's why I decided to become an enforcer. To make sure there was justice in our world."

"That sounds good, but how am I supposed to know you're not making empty promises?"

"You can't be sure. You don't know me. No matter how many times I promise this to you, it's not going to change that. But this is the only way for James *and* you to be free. And while I don't know you, it's pretty obvious that you care for James and that you want him to be safe. The only way to obtain that is to tell me the truth."

Oscar wanted to. He wanted to get that weight off his shoulders, off his soul. He wanted to say the words out loud and atone for the fact that he hadn't done anything to stop what had happened. But he still had doubts. "You're only one man. What will you do if I tell you that my father was behind all this? You could try arresting him, but he's going to resist, and while you might be stronger than him, he has the pack behind him."

"I'm not going to arrest him." Oscar jerked back, and Ignatius rushed to add. "Yet. Not yet, Oscar. You're right, I'm only one man, and trying to arrest your father wouldn't go well for me. But I *can* go back to my team and talk to my team leader, tell him what happened and that I believe your father is guilty of killing Alpha Torres. That means we'll come back with the entire team and make sure he pays for what he did, one way or another." Ignatius hesitated. "I understand why you're wary. The conclave doesn't have prisons. We're only called when the crimes warrant death, and that means that once we've arrested him, we'll have to execute your father. It's not something anyone should have to see."

"I don't care about that."

"He's your father."

Ignatius didn't seem to understand. Oscar might have cared, before. He'd tried too hard for so long to be what his father wanted him to be, what he needed him to be — or rather, what Oscar had thought his father needed him to be.

Not anymore. Oscar had had enough of being beaten, of being *whipped* for doing the right thing. Whatever his father needed, it wasn't what Oscar needed, or wanted, and he was done. "Can you take me away?"

Ignatius blinked. "What?"

"If I tell you what happened, what *really* happened, you'll leave. You just said so yourself. I want to go with you. I can't afford my father to even suspect what I told you, because he'd kill me then, and without me, you don't have the confirmation that what James said is true."

"He's your father. Surely—"

"He whipped me himself when he found out I was the one who'd let James go."

Ignatius' eyes widened. "Whip you? Is that why he keeps saying you're not feeling well?"

"In part. I haven't been allowed to leave my room since it happened. In the beginning, I couldn't have, but now, he just wanted to make sure I don't tell people what happened. He wants to keep an eye on me, control me. What do you think he will do if he finds out I told you he killed Alpha Torres and blamed James for it?"

Ignatius didn't have to think about it to know the answer to that question. If Becket had whipped his own son—the sweet man who was looking at Ignatius with his big brown eyes—just because Oscar had opened the door to James' cell, he wouldn't hesitate to do it again if he realized he might be about to die. Ignatius wouldn't be surprised if Becket tried to take his son to Hell with him, and that wasn't something he was ready to let happen. Oscar was trying to do the right thing, and he shouldn't pay with his life for that.

"Tell me what happened," Ignatius said. He moved his fingers up Oscar's leg and wrapped his hand around Oscar's ankle. He could feel the bone pressing against his skin, the tickle of hair, the warmth of the flesh. Oscar didn't move away, but he did look down. Ignatius wasn't sure what he was doing. He wanted to reassure Oscar that everything was going to be all right, and while he couldn't make that promise, he could do everything in his power to make it happen.

Oscar looked away, out the window. "My father never liked the way Alpha Torres guided this pack. My mother was killed by a bitten wolf who'd lost control when I was four, and since then, he's hated bitten wolves. The fact that a lot of were-wolves believe they're not as good as born wolves doesn't help, and there are so few born wolves left that they'd do just about anything to make sure we don't die out."

"You sound sure that he did it."

"That's because I am." Oscar sighed heavily. "I overheard him talking about it once, a year or so ago. He and his friend were wondering how they could get away with killing Alpha Torres. My father hated that Alpha Torres had welcomed James into the pack, so he decided to use him. I should have done something, told someone, but I didn't know who, or how. My father caught me listening in, and he beat me. It wasn't anything I wasn't used to, but, well, he threatened to do worse to me, so I kept my mouth shut. And when nothing happened, I thought he'd changed his mind. I wasn't going to ask him about it, so instead of telling Alpha Torres, I kept quiet. I thought my father had just been ranting or talking his head off after drinking too much. And then Alpha Torres was found dead."

"And your father made sure James was blamed for it."

"He did. He asked Roger what he'd seen when he'd found the body, and Roger told everyone about the claw marks. Then someone else said they'd seen James lurking around, which is ridiculous because he doesn't lurk. We all walk around pack territory, and the reason James was alone was that he didn't have any friends. We *were* friends, but my father would have been furious if he'd seen us together. But I knew right away that even though he'd been seen around, he didn't have anything to do with Alpha Torres' death. But my father started ranting about bitten wolves who had no control, and everyone knew James didn't. It was easy for him to convince the pack that he'd been the one to kill Alpha Torres."

"And when he was locked up, you freed him."

"Yes. I wasn't sure what you and the rest of your team would do. My father seemed convinced you'd kill him without asking questions, and I couldn't risk that happening. I'm sorry if telling James to run was the wrong thing to do, but I'd do it again if I were in the same situation. Because if you didn't kill James, my father would have to make sure he couldn't talk about what had happened."

Ignatius nodded. "I understand." He really did. Oscar's father was keeping him here in this room because he was aware of the fact that Oscar knew what had really happened. "I don't want to hurt you by asking this, but why hasn't your father made sure you wouldn't be able to talk?"

"You mean, why hasn't he killed me already?"

"Yes. It would be the safest way for him to make sure this doesn't come out. You're a liability."

"I'm also one of his only strengths. He sold me to a nearby pack who wanted a born wolf. I'm supposed to marry the alpha's daughter and have lots of born wolf babies with her."

"It would be a way to get you out of his way. He wouldn't be able to hurt you." The fact that Ignatius didn't like the thought of Oscar marrying a woman and giving her children didn't matter. Oscar's safety mattered, and if Oscar wanted this, then Ignatius would make sure it happened.

Oscar shuddered. "And I wouldn't be able to give that woman babies, no matter how hard I tried. I don't want to go. It would only be another prison for me, and I want to be free. I want to be the one to choose what I want to do with my life and where I want to live it. I know going would keep me safe from my father, but no. I'm staying." He bit his lower lip. "Unless you can offer me an alternative?"

"What did you have in mind?"

"If this goes well, James will be free, right?"

"He will."

"I want to join him. We're friends, and we can stick

together, protect each other, whatever."

Ignatius had to smile at that. "I don't know James, but you do, so I'll trust you on this. But I'm pretty sure James already found someone to protect him. The reason I'm here is mainly that one of my best friends called me. He somehow found James and took him under his wing, and when he heard what had happened, he called me and asked me to look into this. He didn't think the team had done their jobs correctly, and I agree now that I'm here and that I've talked to you, which we didn't the first time around. But we'll change that, and James will be free to stay with Fyfe, if that's what they both want."

Oscar frowned. "Oh. Well, I'm happy he found someone who believed him and who's standing up for him."

"I'm sure Fyfe would do the same for you." He opened his finger to remove his hand from Oscar's ankle, but Oscar grabbed his wrist. His cheeks flushed, but he didn't move away, not even when his expression twisted in pain.

"You're going to go get the rest of your team soon."

"I am. I can't do this alone."

"Take me with you when you go. Please. I promise I won't bug you and that I'll keep up."

Ignatius wanted to say yes. He hated the thought of leaving Oscar here, in his father's hands, especially now that he knew what Becket was ready to do to his son. "He's going to realize what's happening if we disappear at the same time."

"He will. Does it matter, though? He already knows you suspect something is off."

"He might run."

"He won't. He wants the pack. He wants to control it, to use it as he pleases, to mold it the way he thinks it should be. He's not going to abandon that. He's going to find a way around my disappearance and what you found out. He's going to say that James and I were lovers and that we organized Alpha Torres' death together, that we were planning to use him as a scapegoat the entire time."

"You and James weren't lovers."

"Never. But he was my friend."

"That doesn't change what happened." Ignatius frowned. "You know that the enforcers make the final decisions in these cases."

"Like judges. I know."

"My team trusts me. Even if a few might decide they're not sure that your father was the one who killed Alpha Torres, my word has its weight, and I believe you. I believe you, and they'll believe me, no matter what he says. They all try to find a way out of what awaits them when they have to face us, to find excuses, and they all accuse someone else. We're used to that."

"So you'll take me?"

Ignatius couldn't ignore the way Oscar's hand on his skin made him feel. He was probably an asshole for wanting Oscar in his bed, but he did, there was no denying that. There also was no denying the fact that Oscar would be in danger if he stayed with the pack. His father might be a cruel fool, but he wasn't an idiot. He knew that Ignatius suspected him, and he'd make sure Ignatius wouldn't find Oscar again when he came back, just in case that was enough for him to save his skin.

Ignatius nodded. "You'll come with me. I'm not leaving you here on your own."

"I'd like to see your wounds if that's okay with you."

Oscar blinked. "Why?"

"Has your father brought in a healer?"

"No."

"A doctor? Has anyone looked at them at all? Given you painkillers or antibiotics?"

"No."

Ignatius nodded. "That's what I thought. I want to make sure they're not getting infected and that you won't have a problem when we leave. There's no way to tell if we'll have to run or not, but I doubt your father is just going to let you walk away, so we'll probably have to sneak you out of this bedroom. You can't climb off the roof if you're in pain."

Oscar had gotten used to the pain—which wasn't something he'd ever thought could happen—but he could see Ignatius' point. It wouldn't just be his life he'd put at risk if he wasn't able to move because of infection, but also Ignatius', and that wasn't something he wanted to risk.

He looked at the door, then down at Ignatius' wrist. He was still holding it, which meant that Oscar's father couldn't hear either of them. Oscar had a hard time believing that, but he knew Ignatius hadn't been lying. Otherwise his father would have barged into the bedroom as soon as Oscar had told Ignatius he was the one who'd killed Alpha Torres.

"Well, it shouldn't be a problem if he can hear you. Maybe invent something or fake a conversation with me. I'll keep as quiet as I can. Do you have anything to clean the wounds?"

"In that cupboard." Oscar was used to taking care of himself, cuts and bruises included, but none of them had ever been on his back. He couldn't reach those, and he suspected at least some of the wounds were infected because of the pain and how the skin pulled when he moved. He should have asked for help a while ago, but he knew better. His father wouldn't let him die, but he also wouldn't go out of his way to make sure Oscar was comfortable. It was part of his punishment, and Oscar's pain had never mattered much to his father anyway.

"I'm going to touch your ankle again," Ignatius said once he was back with a bottle of disinfectant and some gauzes, his fingertips on the skin of Oscar's neck.

The sensation made Oscar feel flush and his stomach churn. "That doesn't make sense."

"What?"

"I need to turn around so you can get to my back. Let me go. I'll face the wall and take my t-shirt off. Then I'll start talking about what I didn't see as if I were having a conversation with you while you check the wounds." He hesitated. "I don't know if I'll need you to touch me. I mean, if it hurts, I might cry out, and that would give my father a reason to come in."

"I'll make sure to keep my hands on you." Ignatius' eyes widened. "You know what I mean."

Oscar smiled. "I do." This wasn't what he'd expected when his father had told him about the conclave enforcer. Ignatius was nothing like he'd thought he would be, and Oscar wasn't sure if that was a good thing or not.

Ignatius' fingers trailed away from Oscar's neck. Oscar cleared his throat and turned around, facing the wall like he'd said he would. He reached for the bottom of his t-shirt, hissing only a bit as Ignatius helped him pull it off.

"I don't know what happened to Alpha Torres," he said loud enough that his father would hear him if he was still out there. "I swear. I didn't even see his body. I wasn't around the day he died."

He twisted his heck to watch Ignatius, and he knew things weren't good from the frown on the vampire's face. "Do you need anything else from me? I'm tired, and as my father told you, I haven't been feeling well."

Ignatius cupped Oscar's shoulder with one hand. "There's some infection in the deepest wound. I'm going to clean them, and it's going to hurt. I have antibiotics in my bag, but they'll have to wait until tomorrow. I'll make sure you get them, though. You need to take them if you want the infection to fade."

"I'll take them." Oscar wasn't going to let his father ruin

his life more than he already had.

It wasn't easy to keep up a stream of meaningless conversation while Ignatius cleaned the wounds. Oscar's skin felt tight and painful, even though Ignatius was incredibly careful about his movements and what he did to Oscar. Oscar knew it would be worse in a few hours—he'd be asleep by then, and he'd probably try to roll to his side or his back. He'd done that a few times and the pain had woken him up.

But through the pain and humiliation at the thought that Ignatius knew how those wounds had appeared on Oscar's back, Oscar admitted to himself that it had been a while since he'd last felt this *safe*. As far as he remembered, he'd never felt this way, not with anyone. Maybe with his mother, but she'd died twenty years ago. Oscar had grown up being afraid of angering his father, and that hadn't changed.

What was it about Ignatius that made him feel safe and like everything—or almost everything—was right in the world? Well, except for the pain in his back, but he'd had his fair share of pain in life, and he'd survive this, too.

Ignatius' touch became more soothing. "I'm done," he said, stroking a stripe of skin at the bottom of Oscar's back where his father hadn't hit him.

"How bad is it?"

"I've seen worse, but I hate that you had to go through this."

Ignatius was so freaking sweet. "I'm used to this." Oscar wanted Ignatius to continue touching him, but he felt vulnerable half-naked, so he grabbed his t-shirt and held it against his chest even though Ignatius couldn't see that part of him.

"I hate that you're used to it, too. No one should live this way."

"Luckily for me, I won't have to much longer."

"Right." Ignatius' hand dropped away.

Oscar hurried to put his t-shirt back on and turned to face

the vampire. His back hurt more than before because Ignatius had cleaned the wounds, but Oscar bit on his lower lip so he wouldn't cry out because he'd moved too fast. "Thank you," he whispered.

Ignatius took his hand. "Don't thank me yet. I can't promise you anything, but I don't like the thought of leaving you behind, so I'll do what I can. I still need to talk to the other two witnesses we interrogated the first time we came and see if their stories match with what they already told us. The way things went with the first witness, though, I suspect they will. You're the only one who isn't afraid of your father, even though you have more reasons than anyone else to be."

Oscar softly sorted. "Trust me, I *am* afraid of him. But James is my friend, and I don't want to see him hurt. He's already been through enough. Besides, Alpha Torres might still be alive if I'd talked to him, but I was too much of a coward to do it."

"You couldn't put yourself at risk. I'm sure he would have understood."

Oscar wanted to believe that, but he wasn't sure he could.

"I'll leave the antibiotics on your windowsill," Ignatius said, getting up but not letting go of Oscar's hand. "You should try to get some sleep. I'm surprised you're still awake."

"I don't sleep much, or well."

"All right. Still, get some rest, and drink water. You need both to get better. Take the antibiotics and the painkillers I'll leave for you and try not to pull too much on the wounds. I don't want the scabs coming off."

"You're leaving?" Oscar knew it made sense and that his father wouldn't just stand outside his bedroom for the rest of the night, but he didn't want to be alone.

He'd been alone for too long. Ignatius had somehow broken that—broken through the wall Oscar kept between himself and the rest of the world — and Oscar didn't want him to go, not yet.

Not ever, and wasn't that a terrifying thought?

Ignatius wanted to stay with Oscar all night long, but he knew Becket would get suspicious. He was no doubt still right outside the bedroom waiting to find out how this conversation had gone, and he'd barge in eventually if Ignatius didn't come out. "I have to."

Oscar's expression fell. "I know. My father is still out there, isn't he?"

"Probably, although you know him better than I do. But he was nervous about what you were going to tell me, so I suspect he is."

"He came to me earlier." Oscar gestured at his swollen cheek. Ignatius had noticed it when he'd come into the bedroom, but he hadn't said anything, even though the sight had made him want to kill someone. "He warned me about telling you only what he needed me to tell you, keeping to my initial story."

"I'm sorry you had to live with him. No one should raise hands to you."

Oscar smiled slightly. "It's nothing new, but I do hope I'll be able to leave this behind soon."

"I'll do whatever I can to make that happen." Oren would probably be horrified by Ignatius' promise — the conclave enforcers intervened only when the conclave deemed it necessary, like when there was a vampire on the loose feeding on humans and not being careful, or when an alpha was killed. They tended to want to make sure the next alpha was a good one and not the person who'd killed the old one because that never ended well, and that was what they had on their hands in this case. They'd thought they'd had to deal with a new werewolf with no control, but instead, the killer was a born wolf who knew what he was doing, including when he'd tried to make an innocent pay by lying to the enforcers.

The conclave didn't take well to liars. *Ignatius* didn't take well to liars, and Becket was going to realize that.

Ignatius wanted to call Oren and have the team come, but he knew he needed to get Oscar out before Becket realized what was happening and hurt him or shipped him off to that other pack when it clearly wasn't what Oscar wanted.

Ignatius squeezed Oscar's shoulder. "Everything will be all right. I'm going to hole up for the day, but I'll be back tomorrow night, and we'll go talk to my team leader. I'll tell him what happened, and I'm sure the team will come back and take care of your father. Then you'll be able to choose what you want to do, if you want to stay with the pack or—"

"No. I'm not staying here, not even after my father is gone. I want to come with you. I want to make sure James is okay, and if he doesn't want anything to do with me, I'll find a new place, start a new life."

Ignatius nodded. That was harder to do than it sounded—he should know considering the number of times he'd had to start over in his long life as a vampire—but if that was what Oscar wanted, he'd do what he could to help. He suspected Fyfe would be more than happy to welcome Oscar into his coven, though, just like he probably had with James. Ignatius was going to need to have a conversation with him about picking up strays, especially strays who'd been accused of brutally murdering their alpha.

Oscar was bundled in his bed when Ignatius left his bedroom. He didn't want to go, but he forced himself to. He schooled his expression so Becket wouldn't know something had happened and strode out, closing the door behind himself.

Sure enough, Becket was leaning against the wall with his

arms crossed over his chest. He jumped when Ignatius left Oscar's bedroom. "What did he tell you?"

"I thought you'd want to know how he is, considering he's not feeling well."

"Of course. I'll go in to check on him as soon as we're done."

"He's asleep." Ignatius didn't want Oscar to have to answer his father's questions, especially not when he was probably feeling more vulnerable than usual. "He fell asleep while we were talking."

"But you got what you needed from him?"

"He confirmed what my team members found out the last time we were here, and what the other witnesses said. I'll talk to the last two of them tomorrow, since I doubt they'll still be awake at this hour of the night, but that shouldn't be a problem." Ignatius smiled, making sure to show Becket his fangs. "I'll be out of your hair by tomorrow night."

"What's going to happen next?"

"I'll talk to my team leader and refer to what happened while I was here. He'll be the one making the decisions, but everything should be fine. I'm sure that by now, Oren has managed to get James to talk, and if he didn't, well, you have four witnesses here who can confirm he was the one who killed Alpha Torres." Lying left a bitter taste in Ignatius' mouth, but this was the only way he could get out of there and take Oscar with him. In normal circumstances, he would have left right now and told Oren they needed to go back and arrest Becket, but he couldn't leave Oscar behind.

Ignatius wasn't even sure why he cared so much. Oscar was sweet and vulnerable, and he was in a terrible situation, but he certainly wasn't the first man or woman Ignatius had met who was. Yet the thought of leaving Oscar behind to deal with his father and possibly be beaten or even whipped again was something Ignatius didn't want to consider, even though it made his job harder. The best thing—the easiest thing—would be to go back now, alone.

Oren didn't know Ignatius was here. Ignatius had told him he wanted to investigate a lead, but that was all he'd said. Oren was used to the team members doing things on their own. All of them were several hundred years old and were experts when it came to defending themselves, attacking, and doing their job. The main reason they had a team leader was that it was easier to deal with the conclave when only one of them had to report to them. Oren was also good at keeping the peace, since the team was made up of more than vampires, but with as old as they all were, they'd learned to deal with the different species even if they had a problem with them. Things were sometimes tense, but nothing Ignatius or any of them couldn't deal with.

Ignatius went back to his bike. He had a first aid kit in there, and he dug it out of the saddlebag, then turned to look at the house. He was sure the doors and windows were all locked up, but that didn't matter since he wasn't planning to go in. He just needed to climb up to Oscar's window and leave him the pills there. Ignatius knew how to do that silently and quickly.

He paused to make sure he wouldn't be interrupted. He could hear that Becket was still up, but from the sound of it, he was in his office at the back of the house. Oscar's bedroom faced the front of the house, so Becket wouldn't hear him. Ignatius secured the pills in his pocket and climbed the side of the house. He slipped a few times, but this was nothing he hadn't done hundreds of times already.

The light was off in Oscar's bedroom, and Ignatius resisted the urge to peek in to make sure he was okay. He didn't want to invade what little privacy Oscar had, even though he didn't think Oscar would mind. Ignatius was weirdly drawn to Oscar, but he suspected Oscar felt the same way toward him. He wasn't sure what it would mean yet, but now wasn't the time to focus on that.

He left the pills on the windowsill and turned to climb down, but the sound of the window opening made him pause.

"Thank you," Oscar whispered.

"Take them. You need it."

"I will. And I'll see you tomorrow evening?"

There was so much hesitation in Oscar's voice, as if he expected Ignatius to have changed his mind, to let him down. "Of course you will." Ignatius turned toward him. He could see Oscar even though it was dark, since he was a predator of the night, and he looked as lovely as he'd been in full light. Acting on instinct and hoping he wasn't about to get punched in the face, Ignatius quickly kissed Oscar's cheek. Oscar gasped, but Ignatius was already backing off. "Take the pills and go to sleep. You'll need it," he said gruffly.

Then he jumped off the roof. He needed to start thinking about what the fuck he was doing with Oscar before he hurt him without meaning to.

CHAPTER THREE

Oscar knew it was psychological, but he was feeling better already, even though he'd only take two pills of antibiotics. But that and the knowledge that he'd soon get out of here made him feel like he could climb a mountain.

Okay, maybe he'd need some help with that, and it would take him way more time than most people, but still. He was ready to leave the pack and his father behind and start a new life, even though he had no idea what was waiting for him in that life. Anything would be better than what he had in this one, though.

Oscar needed to pack some of his things, but he didn't know what. The few things he had from his mother, and some clothes, but he didn't want Ignatius to have to drag too much stuff around, and he didn't know what he'd find when he got wherever he was going. He should probably be able to leave with one backpack, and that made things slightly difficult. He'd spent so much time in his bedroom that he wanted to take everything with him. The stuff in there was his shield against his father and everything wrong in his world, or it had been until now. Oscar wasn't sure what he'd do without it, but he supposed he was going to find out. He had to be careful, though. His father was used to slamming into his bedroom without warning, and the last thing Oscar needed was for him to walk in on him while he was packing.

As if to prove him right, his bedroom door slammed open. He'd been reading, and he put down his book and scrambled to his feet. The movement made him grimace at the pain in his back, and he had to suck in a breath not to cry out. His father would be angry if he showed he was in pain because he didn't want to remember the whipping.

Oscar didn't, either, but he didn't exactly have a choice in that, not with the way his back had been slashed up.

"Have you heard from the enforcer again?" Oscar's father snapped.

"No. I haven't left my room."

"And he hasn't tried to contact you?"

"No." *Shit.* Did he suspect something was off with the story Ignatius had fed him? Of course, Oscar's father was always suspicious. He was such an asshole himself that he was always afraid other people did what he did. He didn't understand that some people were decent and wouldn't whip their kids or try to blame an innocent man for a murder they didn't commit.

Oscar's father pointed his finger at him. "You will. Tell me if he tries to contact you again."

"Of course, Father."

"What did you tell him last night?"

"What you said to tell him. That I didn't know anything except that James was a recently bitten wolf and that he didn't have much control. That while I didn't see anything, it was possible he was the one to kill Alpha Torres."

"Good. See you keep this story up. I won't hesitate to make sure you remember it if you step away from it."

Oscar's back twinged. "I won't forget."

"I wouldn't have had to hurt you if you hadn't let James go in the first place."

"I know."

Oscar's father scoffed. "You've always been too soft-hearted, like your mother."

Oscar was dying to ask about her, but he knew better. His father always got angry when he did, but it made him feel better to know she'd probably have let James go, too. He thought she'd probably have stood up to his father rather than cowering the way he was, but he knew his father wasn't the same man he'd been before she'd died. He didn't want to be whipped again, not when his back hadn't healed yet and his cheek was turning blue from yesterday.

"I doubt the enforcer will come back to talk to you. He already got what he wanted, and he said he was going to leave tonight, after talking to the last two people on his list. Stay in your room and go to bed. That way I know you won't try anything even if he comes around."

"Yes, Father." Little did he know that Ignatius *would* come around and that Oscar had already told him everything he'd wanted to know. His father's time as a free man — as an *alive* man — was coming to an end, but Oscar couldn't tell him that.

Oscar's father left the room without adding anything. Oscar waited until his footsteps faded, then he got up and closed his bedroom door. He hesitated, wondering if he should lock it. It would slow his father down if he came back and give Oscar and Ignatius more time, but he didn't know when Ignatius would arrive, and he didn't want his father to find a locked door if he was still there waiting.

He decided to leave it slightly open so he could hear it if his father came back, then he got out one of his mother's old backpacks from under his bed. That was where he kept his memories of her, so he just needed to add the clothes he liked the most, his toothbrush and a few other toiletries, and his favorite book. The backpack was still light enough that Oscar could carry it without too much of a problem, even with his back still hurting. He'd carry it on his chest, which might be a problem when he had to get off the roof, but it shouldn't be too bad.

Once he was done packing, Oscar hid the bag under his bed again and got into bed. He was still dressed except for his shoes, but he turned the light off. He trusted Ignatius to know he was still awake and to come tonight. Oscar wasn't sure *why* he trusted the vampire, since they didn't know each other, but he had to trust someone, and who better than one of the conclave enforcers? If he couldn't believe what they said, Oscar wasn't sure there was anyone in the world he could trust.

He was half asleep by the time he heard the soft knock on his window. He snapped his eyes open and waited, holding his breath until he heard a second one. He needed to be sure before he got up, because he could still hear his father downstairs. There was no way he'd fallen asleep in front of the TV like he usually did, not with Ignatius still around, and Oscar needed to be careful.

He slid out of bed and went to the door, waiting for a second before closing and locking it. Then he rushed to the window to let Ignatius in.

Ignatius was silent as a cat, slinking in through the window. He landed on the floor without a sound and looked around. "Your father?"

"Downstairs."

Ignatius nodded. "Good. Are you ready?"

"Yes." Oscar's heart was racing, but he *was* ready. He was so ready that he'd throw himself out the window if that meant he could leave this place. He only had terrible memories of the house and pack territory, and he wanted to find a place where he could make good ones.

"Are you sure about this, Oscar? I can't promise you anything. I don't know what you'll find when I take you to James, or if I can make sure you're safe when we get there."

"I'm sure. Any way this goes, I'll still be safer than I am here. You know that."

"You have any questions?"

"I have a lot of them, but I don't think this is the right time or place to ask them. How does this work? Do we just get out through the window and leave?"

"I'm going to help you down and to my bike. You're not going to be able to hide there, obviously, so you'll have to stay in the woods for a few minutes, just the time I need to go tell your father that I'm leaving. I doubt he'll watch me go, but if he does, I'll meet you in the first spot he can't see from the house. Just walk that way. Okay?"

The thought of walking alone in the woods at night wasn't a great one, but Oscar knew he'd be safe. The pack didn't have guards or anything like that. Everyone was asleep except for his father and possibly the two people Ignatius had needed to talk to. Oscar would be safe, even if he was alone. Still, he asked, "Is that necessary?"

"It's a sign of respect. Not that I have a lot of that for your father, but I can't just disappear. I have to tell him I found nothing wrong and hope he believes me. I don't know how he'll react when he finds out you're gone, but I hope he's not going to realize what it means for him."

Oscar wasn't too sure about that, but he couldn't bring himself to care right now.

"Do you have questions? You won't be able to ask them once we're on the bike." Ignatius needed to know if Oscar had thought this through. He could understand the need to leave, since he knew Oscar's situation, but Oscar had to be sure because Ignatius didn't want to get his ass arrested for kidnapping or something. He didn't think that would happen, not after talking with Oscar last night, but still. Anything was possible.

"Where are we going?" Oscar asked, looking at the door.

"Back to the city where we followed James. That's where I left my team, and they're still there. My friend Fyfe also lives there. He's the one who called me to ask me to look into this deeper."

Oscar nodded. "I don't have money."

Ignatius frowned. "What for?" He was worried about staying here too long, but he could still hear Oscar's father moving downstairs, so they should be fine.

"For gas, or a motel room. For a place of my own when we get there."

"We can talk about all that later, but don't worry. We'll find a way. And don't worry about gas or anything else. I never expected you to pay for it."

Oscar bit his lower lip.

He was clearly worried, and while Ignatius understood that, he couldn't give Oscar the time to wrap his mind around everything. "Ready?"

"As ready as I'll ever be." Oscar put his shoes on and dragged a backpack from under the bed. "Let's go."

"That's all you're taking with you?" Ignatius asked, gesturing at the bag. He was relieved, but he didn't want Oscar to leave anything important behind.

"Yes. We're on a bike, so I can't exactly bring more, but there's not much in here that I want to hold on to. Too many bad memories."

Of course. Ignatius should have realized that. "We might be able to come back for more once your father has been dealt with."

"Maybe. It's not that important, though."

"If you say so." Oscar would have time to think about it, so Ignatius didn't push.

He knew how leaving everything behind felt, though. He'd had to do it too many times for him to remember all of them, and none had been easy. Even though Oscar's father was what he was, this was Oscar's home, the only place where he'd lived.

Oscar strode to the window and peered out. "How are we

going to do this?"

"You've never snuck out?"

"No. My father would have been furious, and I like my skin on my back."

Ignatius pressed his lips together. He was *not* going to smile, because it wasn't funny, no matter how Oscar had made it sound. "All right. We'll both get out. Once we're on the edge, I'm going to help you get your feet on the trellis there. I'll hold your hands, but don't worry about being too heavy. You won't be. You just need to get your feet on the trellis and climb down." Ignatius grabbed Oscar's bag before he could put it on his shoulders. He was going to have to once they were on the bike, but for now, Ignatius would carry it.

"I can carry it," Oscar protested.

"I have no doubt, but you need to have free range of movement, and your back hurts. I'll give it back once we on the ground. Ready?"

Oscar was a little pale, and Ignatius could hear his heart race, so he was surprised when Oscar moved even closer to the edge and sat down. He swung his legs off the roof, took a deep breath, and flipped so that his stomach was where his ass had been. Ignatius knelt and grabbed Oscar's hands, then gently lowered him down. "Search with your feet," he murmured.

Oscar's eyes were wide. "I am."

"Stay calm. Nothing's going to happen to you even if you fall. You'll get bruises, but we're not that high." They both knew Oscar's back would hurt like a bitch, but Ignatius didn't mention that. Oscar didn't need to freak out even more than he already was.

Oscar grinned. "Got it. There's something on it."

"Some dead plant."

"Will it hold my weight?"

"It held mine, so I don't think that's going to be a problem.

Now grab the trellis with your free hand."

As soon as both of Oscar's hands were on the trellis, Ignatius jumped. Oscar gasped, but he managed not to scream, something for which Ignatius was grateful. He hadn't thought of telling Oscar he'd jump and that it wouldn't be a problem for him.

He positioned himself under Oscar and helped him down. When his feet were both on the ground, Oscar turned and glared at Ignatius. "You could have told me you'd jump," he said through gritted teeth.

"I forgot. Come on." He took Oscar's hand and pulled him toward the woods. "You know which way to walk?" he asked.

"Follow the road until the house is out of sight and wait for you to arrive."

Ignatius nodded and took the bag off his shoulders. "Don't walk too far. There's no need to. I won't be long." He hated leaving Oscar alone in the dark, but he had to go talk to Becket and tell him he was leaving. He knew Becket would put two and two together once he found out Oscar was gone, but hopefully. By that time, they'd be long gone.

Ignatius walked out of the woods and waited a moment so Oscar had a little time to walk away. Then he climbed the porch steps and knocked on the door.

Becket wasn't happy when he answered. "I'm not letting you talk to my son again. He's exhausted."

Ignatius forced himself to smile. "I'm not here to talk to him again, but to tell you I'm leaving."

Becket blinked. "You are?"

"Yes. All the witnesses repeated what we'd already been told the first time around, so there's no need for me to stay, not when we know what happened. I'm sorry I had to inconvenience you this way." The words tasted bitter coming out of Ignatius' mouth, but they needed to be said.

Becket looked pleased. "I knew this would happen, of course, but I understand you're only doing your job."

"That's right. I go where the conclave sends me. I don't have a choice in that, unfortunately for me, and you."

"I'm just glad you caught James."

Ignatius knew his team had. Oren had texted him and had demanded he come back. Ignatius hadn't answered, because he didn't need Oren to yell at him for what he was doing. Besides, he'd see his team tomorrow night anyway. Oren's scolding could wait another day. "It's one less danger on the streets. Again, I'm sorry for the bother."

Ignatius turned and left. He had to force himself not to run to his bike. He could feel Becket's gaze on his back, so he knew Becket was watching him. He took his time putting on his helmet and getting onto the bike, but he never looked back, not even when he drove away to make sure Becket was still there. If he was on the porch, he wasn't upstairs checking on Oscar, which was a plus.

Ignatius stopped as soon as the house was out of sight. He took his helmet off and looked around, trying to find Oscar, his heart racing at the thought that something had happened to him. Maybe he'd been found by someone? Ignatius knew there were no guards patrolling pack territory, but someone might have been taking a stroll.

Then the bushes rustled, and Oscar came stumbling out of them. Ignatius took his hand and used his power so no one would be able to hear them. "You okay?" he asked.

Oscar nodded. "I'm just not used to walking. My father kept me mostly in my room for the past few months, even when I shifted."

"What an asshole."

That got a surprised chuckle out of Oscar. "So true. So I just need to climb on this thing?"

Ignatius always carried a second helmet, and he'd taken it

out so they'd be out of there as soon as possible. He handed it to Oscar and helped him put it on and fasten it in silence. Oscar's breath hitched a little when Ignatius' fingers brushed against his skin, and Ignatius yearned to lean forward and kiss him. Since Oscar's face was covered, though, he limited himself to raising one of Oscar's hands and place a kiss on his palm. It wasn't something he usually did, and he and Oscar were nowhere so close that it made sense for him to do that, but Oscar didn't pull away. If anything, he swayed closer, and while Ignatius wanted nothing more than to talk about this, they didn't have time. "Climb on."

Oscar was a little wobbly, but Ignatius made sure he knew where to put his feet and that he held onto him well enough that he was secure.

Then they were off.

Oscar had never felt anything like this. He'd been scared of the bike at first. He'd never been on one. He'd barely ever been in a car, since the only times he'd left his house he'd done so in his wolf form. There had been no need for him to leave pack territory, and his father had made sure he didn't.

And now there he was, on the back of a bike, holding onto Ignatius and holding his breath at the novel sensations.

He was free. He still wasn't sure how that had happened, how he'd finally managed to get away from his father, but he was free. He still had no idea what to do with that freedom, what would happen to him, but he had the time to find out. No one would control him ever again. If there was one thing he knew, it was that. He'd make sure of it.

They drove out of pack territory without a problem. Ignatius wasn't going too fast, but there was a certain urgency in the way he drove. There was nothing Oscar could do but hang on for dear life.

He was surprised at how much he trusted Ignatius, and he wasn't sure what to do with that. He didn't know Ignatius, and Ignatius didn't know him, but that kiss he'd given him earlier, and the one from the other night, meant something. Oscar knew that. He might never have been with anyone, might never even have kissed anyone, but he couldn't believe Ignatius was doing this only because he thought it was right. He was a good man, and a conclave enforcer, but while they were known for doing the right thing most of the time, they were also known for staying out of situations they thought didn't involve them. They didn't intervene in cases of abuse, not unless an entire pack or coven was treated badly. Most of them wouldn't have gone out of their way to make sure Oscar was okay, especially when it could complicate the case they were working.

But Ignatius had.

Oscar had no idea what that meant, and he was both afraid and excited about the thought of finding out.

He wasn't sure how long they drove. He recognized a few of the places they passed from what he'd heard during conversations with other pack members, but he didn't want to watch the past pass by. He closed his eyes and pressed his helmet against Ignatius' back, smiling softly and holding on.

When the bike slowed down, he opened his eyes again. He didn't recognize the place where Ignatius was stopping, but there was a motel and a diner that was already open. The sky was starting to brighten, and Ignatius needed to be inside and away from the sun before it hurt him.

"We're stopping for the day?" he asked when Ignatius stopped the bike.

"I have to. I'm mostly covered, but the sun is still uncomfortable."

Oscar didn't mind. He could use some sleep, since he'd barely had any the previous night. He'd been too wound up,

47

knowing what would happen tonight, and after the conversation that he'd had with Ignatius. "Do I have the time to grab something to eat first?" And what about Ignatius? When was the last time he'd eaten?

Ignatius looked around. "I'd rather have you wait inside. I'll go get a room, and once I know you're safe, I'll go get you some food."

Oscar wanted to walk, to experience the world, but Ignatius was right. They were still too close to pack territory, and while his father might not have realized he was gone yet, he would soon. When he got up, he'd go to Oscar's room, and he'd find the door locked and Oscar gone. He'd look for Oscar then, and when he couldn't find him anywhere, he'd realize that Oscar was with Ignatius. That meant he'd also realize that Ignatius knew what had really happened and that he and his team would probably be back soon.

This was a mess, but Oscar didn't think he could have done things differently. The enforcer he'd talked to the first time they'd been in pack territory hadn't been Ignatius, and Oscar wasn't sure he'd have believed him if he'd told him the truth. He still wasn't sure Ignatius' team would intervene and that they would trust that Oscar was telling the truth, but he'd done what he could. He'd told his truth, and things were out of his hands.

Ignatius ushered Oscar into the room he'd gotten, then left.

Oscar looked around. He'd never spent a night in a motel, or in this case, a day, but it was pretty much what he'd expected — two beds, a bathroom tiled in white, bad art on the walls. It was clean, which was more than he'd expected, and while the bed was hard when he sat on it, it was better than sleeping on the ground, or even than sleeping in his old bedroom with his father down the hall.

Oscar's back hurt, and while he wanted to take a shower and wash away all that was left of his old life from his body, he wasn't sure how to deal with the wounds. He couldn't cover them on his own, but maybe he could wash his hair leaning forward? He wanted to be clean when Ignatius came with the food, if anything because Ignatius would need to eat, too, and Oscar was the only source of blood available to him.

Oscar wasn't afraid of letting Ignatius feed on him. He wasn't afraid of Ignatius, period. He trusted the vampire, even though most people would think him crazy. He didn't care what people thought, though. None of them had tried to help him, even though he'd been abused, beaten, and hurt by his father.

He dropped his backpack next to his hip on the bed and twisted to get clean clothes out of it. He'd packed pajama pants, just in case, and he was glad he had.

It was tricky to shower and wash his hair while making sure water didn't get on his back. He knew Ignatius would probably want to check the wounds before they went to bed, even though they didn't hurt as much as they had before. The antibiotics he'd been taking were working, and it was a re-lief — so much so that tears prickled Oscar's eyes.

The only place he'd ever allowed himself to cry was in the shower. No one could hear him under the sound of water, and that was the one place where he was left alone without the possibility of someone walking in on him. His father never had, and he didn't think Ignatius would, either, even if he came back before he was done.

Oscar couldn't sit down and lean against the wall like he usually would, so he pressed his forehead against the tiles and closed his eyes. His back was mostly dry, but water dripped from his hair down to his body, and it felt like its warmth was taking away all the pain and bad feelings Oscar had held onto for so long.

They'd been the only things he'd had for so long, the only things he'd allowed himself to feel. He hadn't let himself hope, because that hope had always been squashed. He hadn't let himself think about a better future.

But now he could, and he had no idea what he'd do.

Oscar felt better once he left the shower. He was careful of his back when he dried himself, and even more so when he dressed. He looked tired when he looked at his reflection in the mirror, and he couldn't deny that sleeping for the next twelve hours sounded damn good. He'd never let himself truly rest at home because his father might come in at any time to pull him out of bed and hurt him.

Oscar blinked when he saw Ignatius sitting on the second bed, a brown bag that smelled amazing in his hands. He smiled at Oscar and held it out. "I wasn't sure what you wanted, so I stuck with a classic burger with fries. I also bought a few bottles of water. I figured you'd need to stay hydrated and whatnot."

The water would no doubt come in handy to help with the blood loss after Ignatius fed on him. "Thank you."

Oscar carefully sat on his bed and opened the bag. The burger smelled heavenly, and it took him no time at all to wolf it down. He slowed down for the fries and looked at Ignatius as he ate them one by one. "What about you?"

"Me?"

"When did you last feed?"

Ignatius' eyes widened. "Oscar—"

"It's a simple question. When did you last feed?"

"That's never a simple question."

"Maybe not. But you do need blood, don't you?"

That wasn't a question Ignatius wanted to answer. He already knew what Oscar was planning. He could tell, even though he barely knew Oscar. But Oscar was a good man, someone who cared for others even though he probably shouldn't. "I'm not going to feed on you."

Oscar cocked his head. "Why not?"

"Because you're still in pain. Because you don't deserve it."

"What don't I deserve?"

"For me to feed from you."

Oscar frowned. "I don't understand. I'm volunteering. You need food, and I have it. How different is that from you going to the diner to buy me this burger?"

"Well, you didn't have to bite me to get it."

"Is it too intimate for you to want that with me?"

To be honest, the thought of biting Oscar and taking blood from him made Ignatius want to push him against the bed and do it. It wasn't usually that way — Ignatius was more than able to feed on people without getting hard or associating it with sex or affection. He didn't think he could do that with Oscar, though.

He liked Oscar, more than he should, considering the situation. He also knew Oscar was incredibly vulnerable right now. He'd been abused most of his life. He didn't have friends or a family to support him. Right now, he saw Ignatius as the only person he could trust in his life and taking advantage of that wouldn't be right. Just the thought made Ignatius' skin crawl.

He shook his head. "I can't." He was hungry, but not *that* hungry.

Oscar frowned. "Why not, though? If it's not intimacy that's the problem, what is?"

"After what you've been through, the last thing you need is for me to take your blood."

"Ah. I see. You think I'm only offering because I think I owe you or something."

"You'd still be with your father if it weren't for me."

Oscar grimaced. "Probably. That doesn't mean I'd do something I don't want to do to thank you. You need blood. I have blood. I'm offering it to you. Unless you have a good reason not to drink it, I don't see why you're refusing. I wouldn't offer if I wasn't okay with it, I promise. I'm done doing things I don't want to do. This is a new chapter in my life, and I'm going to live it the way I want to, me, not anyone else. So, do you want my blood or not?"

"I shouldn't."

"You also shouldn't have taken me away from the pack. Hell, you shouldn't have come back to investigate this. Yet you did."

Why was Oscar making saying *no* so difficult? "You'll regret it later."

"Again, who are you to tell me that? Has everyone you've ever bitten regretted it?"

"Of course not. But they weren't in your situation."

Oscar rolled his eyes. "Look, I can't force you to feed from me. I want you to, though. Not because I owe it to you, but because I want to do something nice for you. I also want you to be at your best when we get wherever it is you're taking me tomorrow. We both know what's coming isn't going to be easy, but especially not for you. You're going to have to face the rest of your team and possibly part of the conclave. Do you really want to do that feeling weak?" He put down the bag he was still holding and cleaned his fingers on a napkin. He held out his hand, tilting it down to expose the inside of his wrist. "You don't have to drink at my neck, right?"

Ignatius swallowed. "No." It was tempting, especially now that Oscar had explained why he was doing it. Ignatius wasn't sure he should believe him, but Oscar was an adult, and even with what had happened to him in the past, he seemed to be convinced of what he was doing. Besides, he wasn't wrong when he said Ignatius needed to be strong tomorrow when they got to the conclave building where Oren had no doubt taken James.

Ignatius sighed. "I hate this."

Oscar grinned and wiggled his wrist. "Maybe, but you still have to eat, and there's food right there. I even showered to be sure you wouldn't be bothered by my smell."

Ignatius gently took Oscar's hand. "You don't smell bad. You didn't before, either." He pressed his nose against the skin of Oscar's wrist and took a deep breath.

Oscar shuddered, and Ignatius had to keep a smile from showing on his face. They were both affected by this, and Ignatius suspected it was for the same reason. Now wasn't the moment to do anything about it, though. No matter what Oscar was saying and what he thought, he *was* vulnerable, and tired, and probably in pain. He needed to sleep now that he'd eaten. They'd be safe for the day, since Ignatius had made sure to hide his bike and to pay with cash. So even if Becket had already realized his son was gone, he wouldn't be able to find them. This was the safest place for them, and tomorrow, once they were back in the city, things were going to get crazy. The last thing they both needed was also to try to deal with whatever was between them. Those feelings weren't going anywhere, and they could wait to deal with them until the most urgent things had been taken care of.

"Still sure of this?" he asked without moving.

"Very much so." He hesitated. "Is it going to hurt?"

"Some." Ignatius didn't remember when he'd been turned. Not only had hundreds of years passed, but it had been on a battlefield. He'd gone down human, thinking he was about to die, and he'd woken up with his skin burning under the sun, a vampire who had no idea what he was or how it had happened. But he'd bitten enough people since then to know that no matter how careful he was, the bite was always going to be painful, and he didn't want to lie to Oscar.

He did his best to be quick about it, slicing through Oscar's skin and sucking on the blood that welled from the wounds.

Oscar sucked in a breath, but he didn't try to move his wrist away. He let Ignatius suckle on the wounds until Ignatius had enough.

He didn't know that Ignatius could have continued to drink, that he *should* have, because the amount he'd taken wasn't nearly enough for him to be satisfied. But Oscar needed his blood as much as he did, and they couldn't waste time tomorrow evening. Oscar was already pale as it was, even with the food he'd eaten. Ignatius wasn't going to put him at risk of fainting or of slowing them down so much that his father caught up to them.

Ignatius licked the wounds clean, letting his saliva start the healing process. He might have taken more care than was strictly necessary, but he didn't want to let go of Oscar just yet. He didn't know if they'd ever share something like this again, and with the strength of Oscar's werewolf blood running in his body, he felt particularly close to Oscar right now. "Still okay?" he asked.

Oscar nodded. He was still pale, maybe a bit more than before, but otherwise, he looked okay. "I didn't expect it to be like that."

Ignatius didn't ask how it had been. He could imagine. He dropped Oscar's hand. "You should go to bed. I'm going to go take a shower. We're safe here. Your father can't find us, even if he's looking for you."

"I know. I trust you."

"Good."

Ignatius still didn't waste time in the shower. He rushed through it, cleaning up just enough that he wouldn't smell. He didn't like the thought of leaving Oscar alone, even if it was only in the other room and only for ten minutes.

But Oscar was still there when Ignatius rushed out of the bathroom. From the looks of it, he'd decided to try to wait for Ignatius to go to bed. He'd stretched out on his bed, stomach down, and had tried to read a book, which was now on the floor next to the bed. He'd pushed the blanket away, but Ignatius raised it and covered him, gently pushing his feet under it.

Oscar didn't even react.

CHAPTER FOUR

Oscar knew he was staring. He also knew it was useless to try to stop. He'd never manage it.

He'd known about the conclave since he was a kid. His father often ranted about them and their power, how he thought they overreached into business that wasn't theirs. Oscar had always thought that there had to be good people in the conclave and that, as his father's behavior showed, it was obvious that the paranormal world *needed* someone to police them and to protect humans from dangers they didn't even know existed.

But he'd never met anyone who was part of the conclave or who worked for them until Alpha Torres died, and he had to admit he wasn't happy with the work they'd done then. That didn't stop him from staring now that he and Ignatius were in a building that belonged to the conclave.

The place was huge, yet Ignatius seemed to know exactly where he needed to go. He'd pulled Oscar along when he'd walked in, and he still hadn't released his hand. Oscar was glad, because he was pretty sure he'd have gotten lost otherwise.

The thought was terrifying. Everything about their situation was scary, and the fact that Oscar's back hurt like hell today wasn't helping. He suspected it was the time on the bike, or maybe the day spent on the hard mattress at the motel. Whatever the reason, he felt like he could have torn off the skin on his back and feel less pain.

"We're just going to talk to Oren," Ignatius said without

slowing down or looking at Oscar. "Then I'll take you home."

"I don't know where home is, though."

"Shit. Okay, I'll take you to a hotel, or maybe I'll ask Fyfe if he knows of a place where you can stay. I'd offer the room I have here, but they're open to all the enforcers who might need it, so it's not really mine, and people who aren't enforcers shouldn't stay here."

"I'll be okay. I can find my way." Except he had no money, no phone, and no friends. But he was far away from his father now, and he'd do whatever he had to do to make sure he stayed far away from him.

"Ignatius," a voice boomed.

Oscar tensed—and his back burned. He swore and gritted his teeth, but he knew the pain was evident on his face when Ignatius turned toward him and frowned. "Oscar?"

"Oscar?" the man who'd spoken asked. "He wouldn't be the new alpha's son, would he?"

Ignatius gently wrapped an arm around Oscar's shoulders. "He would, and he's in pain."

The man—Oscar was pretty sure it was Ignatius' team leader. He remembered him being in pack territory, but luckily, he'd never had to talk to him—pinched the bridge of his nose. "Please tell me I'm not going to get a call from his father telling me his son disappeared overnight."

Ignatius didn't look sorry. "You probably will, actually, but Oscar came willingly, and he knows what happened to Alpha Torres. Just listen to him, Oren. I know I should have acted differently, but we both know it was impossible, because it would have gone against the orders we had. Now hopefully with what I found—"

"A different conclave member took over the case. We don't have the order to execute James Beltran on sight anymore. Which is a good thing, since he's here."

Oscar and Ignatius already knew that, because Ignatius's

friend had called them when James had been taken.

Oren sighed. "Why don't we go inside? We can work on solving this part of the problem. We'll talk about your insubordination later, Ignatius."

Oren turned, and Ignatius followed him, gently tugging Oscar along. He was so careful when he touched Oscar, but that didn't help with the pain, unfortunately. Oscar couldn't wait to be able to stretch on a comfortable bed and sleep, but he wasn't sure when that would happen.

Oscar blinked at James when he walked into the room after Oren. He'd expected his friend to be handcuffed to the table or something, but instead, he was in the lap of a handsome man with a braid. He slid off when he noticed Oscar, and he took a step forward. "Oscar?"

Oscar forced himself to smile, but really, he felt like he was breaking inside. "Hey, James. Still in trouble, huh?"

Oscar didn't want to have to go over what had happened again, but most of all, he didn't want to talk about what his father had done to him. He had to, though.

Ignatius helped him lower himself into one of the empty chairs, and Oscar listened to him and Oren talk about what had happened when Ignatius had left, apparently without telling Oren.

Oscar sighed. "My father was the pack's beta. He's been the beta for decades, and he'd been talking about becoming alpha one day more often every year. I didn't pay attention to it when I was a kid, but as I grew up, I saw how cruel he was." He'd experienced it on his own skin so often that he still bore the scars. "I also knew from the beginning that he was plotting against Alpha Torres. I tried to warn him, but my father beat me." He should have done more, though. He should have at least *tried* to do more.

Oscar swallowed. "I wasn't able to tell Alpha Torres what was going on. When nothing happened, I thought my father had decided it wasn't worth it, or that maybe he didn't have the guts to go through with it. I should have known better. He was just waiting for the perfect scapegoat."

"And he got me," James said. He didn't sound angry, and Oscar was so glad for that. He *knew* he should have done more, but he was doing it now, and he hoped it wasn't too late.

"Yes. He—he found out you and I were friends. I think that's one of the reasons he decided to blame this on you. I'm sorry, James." God, Oscar had hated his father for so long, but he did so especially right now. He wanted the man to die a painful death and to pay for all the pain he'd caused.

Oscar was only mildly surprised when James patted his shoulder. He'd always known James was a good man, and he could have wept at the thought that James wasn't going to hold this against him. "Don't worry about it. This wasn't your fault, only your father's."

Oscar nodded. "I know. He killed Alpha Torres," he said, looking at Oren, who hadn't yet said anything. "I wasn't there when he did it, but I know he did, because he talked about how he'd set James up for it and how James was going to be killed. He hates James because he's a bitten wolf. I know you might not believe me, but—"

"I do. And since Ignatius was away for so long, I suspect he gathered evidence."

Oscar blinked. He'd thought Ignatius was only there to talk to the witnesses, but of course, he hadn't followed Ignatius around.

Everything was a blur after that. Oren and Ignatius started talking, and after making sure that Oscar was at least eighteen and that his father wouldn't be able to complain he'd been kidnapped, Oren dismissed him.

Oscar had no idea what to do now, since Ignatius was supposed to stay and talk to Oren, but he'd barely thought that far when Fyfe stepped in.

"And he's going to become one of my coven members," Fyfe said.

Oscar was too tired to protest or to even begin wrapping his mind around what that meant for him. He was grateful for the protection and the fact that he wouldn't have to find a place to stay right now, though.

"I have to stay and talk to Oren," Ignatius told Fyfe. Oscar was pretty sure he'd missed part of the conversation, but now that he'd said what he had to say, he was crashing. Years of not sleeping well, or eating even worse, and of being beaten, were crowding upon him, and he had no idea how to deal with them.

He'd wanted freedom, and he had it. He hadn't expected his old life to cling to him the way it was, though. He'd thought he'd be able to put everything behind as soon as he left, but he'd been wrong.

"We'll take care of him," Fyfe said, his tone serious yet tender. "I promise. And once you're done here, just come to the house. You can have a guest room for as long as you need one."

At least Oscar wouldn't be alone in this new world of his, not for long. He was going to have to learn to be without Ignatius sooner or later, but that was something he'd worry about later.

"I should kick your ass to the curb and call it a day," Oren said.

He was leaning against the table in the interrogation room with his arms crossed over his chest. For the first time ever, Ignatius was in the chair that was usually used by suspects. He didn't like it, and he hoped Oren wasn't looking at him as a suspect, even though he *had* taken things into his own hands rather than going to Oren with his doubts and asking him what they should do.

Ignatius cleared his throat. "I know."

"You should have talked to me."

"I know."

Oren rubbed his forehead. "I already suspected the beta had done it."

"Alpha Becket now."

Oren snorted. "He didn't waste time. I'm not surprised. What proof do you have?"

Ignatius leaned back. "Nothing concrete, unfortunately. I talked to the witnesses, including Oscar. The other three repeated what we'd been told the first time around, word for word, so I'm pretty sure they learned that by heart and just went with it. And of course, there's Oscar. He doesn't have physical proof of what his father did, but I believe him. I trust him."

"And since I'll be the one to make the decisions whether Becket is guilty or not, that won't be a problem."

That was how the conclave and its enforcers worked. Their justice was more brutal than human's. They couldn't afford to put people in jail and give them a trial, but every enforcers' team was made of several different paranormal creatures. The leader was the one who went over the proof they gathered and decided whether the person they were investigating was guilty and what the punishment would be. Since the conclave was brought in only when the circumstances were dire and when there was more than one kind of creature involved, the punishment was usually death. It depended on the circumstances, though.

"I want to go back," Oren said.

"I thought you would."

"Without you."

Ignatius wasn't surprised, and he was relieved. Oscar had

to be lost, even though he was with friends, and Ignatius wanted to be there for him to give him whatever he needed to get used to this new life of his. Besides, he doubted Becket would be happy to see him. He'd not only gone there under false pretenses—he'd also taken his son away from him. Even though Oscar had wanted it and would probably have found another way to leave if Ignatius hadn't takin him along, Becket was going to view this as a kidnapping, and Ignatius' presence there would only make things worse.

"I know you did most of the work on this, but considering everything—"

Ignatius raised his hand. "I get it, and it's not a problem. Honestly, I'm not looking forward to seeing Becket again, and I know that my presence there would make what is already a mess an even bigger one."

Oren nodded. "Good."

"What will you do once you're there?"

"Pack Oscar's stuff, for one. I'll also talk to the other three witnesses again, but I know how you work, so I doubt I'll find anything you haven't found already."

"So you'll take care of him."

"Yes. It's pretty clear-cut at this point, to be honest. Like I said, I already suspected he was the one behind this. The only reason I couldn't go after him was that the conclave member in charge of this investigation wanted us to focus on James."

"Has that changed?"

Oren chuckled. "No, but we're not working with him anymore. I don't know how your friend managed it, but Maurice managed to push him aside and take his place. He doesn't have a grudge against werewolves, and he agreed to let me take the lead for real this time."

Ignatius was going to have to find Fyfe a present. He didn't know what yet, but knowing Fyfe, it was going to have to be big and possibly golden. "That's good."

"Of course it is. And I'll keep what you did from the conclave. They don't need to know."

"Thank you. Do you need anything else from me?"

"Actually, I do. As I said, I'm going to talk to those witnesses again. I hope they'll agree to talk once I make it clear that Becket won't be able to hurt them if they do, but that still leaves us one problem. You said Becket doesn't have a beta yet, right?"

Ignatius briefly closed his eyes. "He doesn't, and that means there won't be anyone to take his place once you execute him."

"There won't, and that's going to be a problem."

"You can choose a temporary alpha."

"You're right, I can. But I have no idea who would be a good pick. And since Oscar is Becket's son . . ."

"That makes him the next alpha once his father is gone." Ignatius groaned. "He's not going to be happy about it."

"You don't think he wants that?"

"I *know* he doesn't want it. His life with the pack has been hell, Oren. I don't know what kind of man Alpha Torres was, and while it was great of him to give James a place to live and learn how to control his wolf, he also closed an eye on the abuse Oscar had to go through at the hands of his father, the pack's *beta*. So no, Oscar doesn't want to go back, possibly never. But I'll talk to him about this, okay? I'll ask him what he thinks, who would make the best alpha."

"You need to convince him to come back if you can . His word will have more weight if he's there. And he won't be alone if he decides to come."

"I *will* talk to him, but I can't promise you anything." And Ignatius would make sure Oscar didn't go back if he didn't want to. He deserved to be happy and to be able to make his own choices. That wouldn't happen if the conclave forced him to go back.

But Oren wasn't the conclave, and Ignatius trusted him. He wouldn't force Oscar to do anything against his will.

"I just need you to talk to him," Oren said. "The rest of the team and I are leaving in a few hours. We'll do whatever has to be done, and we'll come back. But we can't leave the pack without an alpha for long, especially after we're the ones to execute Becket. I hope to find someone to put in place, but if I don't, I'll need him if he can stand to help."

"I said I'll talk to him, and I will."

"Good. Give him a few days to settle down, though. He didn't look like he was steady on his feet when he was here, and I got a sample of how overwhelming your friend Fyfe can be. He's a handful."

Ignatius laughed. "That he is. But he helped us with this case. So I won't hold it against him." He *would* ask Fyfe a few questions, though, like why James Beltran had been in his lap when they'd walked into the interrogation room. Ignatius had suspected that there was more to Fyfe's request that he look into the case than he'd thought, and he was sure of it now.

Trust Fyfe to pick up a stray werewolf accused of murder and fall in love with him.

Ignatius shouldn't be surprised. He knew Fyfe better than most, since they'd spent a few decades together before he'd become a conclave enforcer. He knew what made Fyfe tick, and he knew that Fyfe had a protective streak a mile wide. He'd probably found James and had thought he looked like an adorable puppy or something.

Oren patted Ignatius' shoulder. "Go get some rest, or as much rest as you can manage to get in a house where Fyfe is. You deserve it. You might not have gone about this the right way, but you did it from the right place, and I suspect that you got a lot more than you expected in return."

"I have no idea what you're talking about." But He couldn't deny to himself that he felt way more for Oscar than he should be feeling.

He liked Oscar, and maybe Fyfe wasn't the only one with a protective streak in him. Ignatius wanted to protect Oscar and make sure that his second chance at life went well. It didn't matter if Oscar wanted him in this life or not. Ignatius just needed him to be happy — and if it *was* with him, then so much better.

Oscar had no idea what to do.

Someone — he was pretty sure the man's name had been Aubrey, but he wouldn't swear on it — had shown him to an empty guest room, then had disappeared to give Oscar time to settle in. And Oscar had. Even though he had no idea how long he was going to stay there, he'd unpacked his bag to try to give himself a hint of normality.

What now, though? Oscar was tired, but he knew better than to think he'd be able to sleep before Ignatius came back. *If* Ignatius came back. Oscar had no idea what was going to happen to Ignatius, since he'd gone to pack territory without authorization and taken the investigation into his own hands.

So sleep was out. Oscar was kind of hungry, but he was more than a little aware of the fact that the house he was in belonged to a coven. A *vampire* coven, while he was a were-wolf, and a born wolf at that. Those two categories didn't mix. If anything, they were explosive when they tried to, and Oscar didn't want to create problems for Fyfe, who had so nicely opened his home to him. Of course, the fact that Oscar was surrounded by vampires — and James — didn't mean they didn't want him there. It was true vamps and wolves didn't usually mix, but he and Ignatius hadn't had a problem getting along, and from what Oscar had seen, neither had Fyfe and James.

He could probably stay in his new bedroom until Ignatius

came back, especially since he wasn't even sure he'd find something to eat in the house. Vampires ate blood, as the slight ache in his wrist reminded him of. He didn't care about that, and he didn't have strong feelings about it except those he'd experienced when Ignatius had fed on him, and those were all positive, although that was no doubt because it had been Ignatius.

So was there food he could eat in the house? Maybe. James looked like he lived there, and he didn't feed on blood. There had to be stuff for him around, right? And there was only one way for Oscar to find out—he'd have to leave the bedroom and face whoever was waiting for him out there.

No one was. When Oscar opened the bedroom door and peeked out, the hallway was empty. He remembered the way to the front door, but once he was there, he had no idea where to go. He'd have asked someone, but the house felt like it was empty, and considering how big it was, he found it a bit creepy. It was the middle of the night, so there should be someone around, right?

Oscar cleared his throat. "Anyone there?" he asked. He should probably have used a louder voice, but he felt like something bad might happen if he did, like in the few horror movies he'd watched.

"To your right. Well, I don't know which way you're facing, so just follow my voice," Fyfe answered from somewhere in the house.

Oscar obeyed and followed his voice. He had no idea where he was going, but Fyfe kept up a steady stream of conversation, even though Oscar wasn't answering and had no idea who the people he was talking about were.

Fyfe was sitting at the counter in a vast kitchen when Oscar found him. He had his computer in front of him, but he looked up when he heard Oscar, and he smiled at him. "Hungry?"

Oscar shuffled. "Yes. I'm sorry."

Fyfe blinked. "Why are you sorry? You're a werewolf. You need to eat food. And you're lucky James got here before you did, because it means we do have food around. Just check the fridge and the cupboards and take out whatever you want."

Oscar opened the fridge and blinked at the opaque lined bottles in it. More than half the fridge was filled with them, and it was one of the biggest he'd ever seen. He hadn't even known a fridge this big existed.

"Oh, and ignore the bottles of blood. James made the mistake of sniffing one of them once, and he almost puked."

Oscar stayed as far away as possible from the bottles as he could and took out a block of cheese and butter. "Do you have bread?" he asked as he placed the food on the counter.

"In one of the cupboards. James loves bread."

Oscar smiled. "He does, doesn't he? I remember him always having a sandwich in his hands."

"He still does, although sometimes, he has *me* in his hands now."

Oscar would have choked if he'd already been eating. "I . . . see."

Fyfe chuckled. "Sorry. I know it takes some time to get used to me and my big mouth. James has told me often enough. But you have that time, and in the meantime, just tell me if I say something inappropriate."

"That *was* kind of weird." Oscar found the bread and opened the first drawer he found, happy to see knives in it. "So are you and James together?" he asked once he was back at the counter. The fact that James had been in Fyfe's lap earlier pointed to that, but he wanted to be sure so he could avoid saying stupid things. Fyfe didn't look like he didn't want to talk about it, so Oscar thought he'd ask.

"We are."

"Isn't it weird?"

"You mean because he's a wolf, and I'm a vampire?"

"That, and the fact that he was accused of murder when you met him."

Fyfe closed his laptop and leaned back in the stool he was sitting on. "Well, I never believed he'd killed someone. He doesn't have it in him, and trust me, I've met my fair share of killers while I was human and even more after I got turned."

"So you knew he was innocent even though you didn't know him. That was a huge risk to take."

Fyfe shrugged. "I'm a risk taker. That's kind of how I ended up being the leader of this coven. I never intended to be responsible for anyone other than myself, yet here I am." He opened his arms. "Although it's not all bad. I wouldn't have been able to help James if I hadn't been the coven leader."

"And no one will mind having me in the coven?" Oscar wasn't exactly looking forward to being part of this kind of thing after his life in the pack, but he was a werewolf, and they were made to live in packs. He also didn't have anyone else in his life, and he knew he'd never make it on his own. He didn't *want* to be alone. He wanted a family, a real one, and he was starting to think that maybe he could get that here.

"You know, you and Ignatius are both welcome here," Fyfe said.

"He's your friend."

"He is. Well, we used to have sex, but it's been a few hundred years. Or has it been less? I can't remember, but don't worry. We're not in love or anything. He's all yours." He beamed, exposing his fangs. "I have James, and he's more than enough for me. But I think James will be happy not to be the only non-vampire around, you know? He's learning to control his wolf from one of my friends, but maybe you could help. You two are already friends, and you were born with that ability."

"I'll do what I can. I wanted to help him from the beginning, but my father . . ."

Fyfe leaned over the counter and patted Oscar's hand. "Don't worry about that, or anything else. You're part of my coven now. I'll announce it soon. You have a home, I'll take care of whatever money you need until you can find a job if that's what you want, and hopefully, we can be a family. Some coven members will be happier than others to have you here, but if anyone says anything, I want you to let me know, okay?"

Oscar nodded. This was overwhelming, but in a good way. He was still relieved once he was done eating and he could go back to his room, though. He still wasn't used to having a reversed schedule, and his eyes were starting to close on their own.

The sleepiness fled Oscar's body when he walked into his bedroom and found Ignatius sitting on the edge of the king-sized mattress.

Ignatius looked up when he heard the door open. He smiled at the sight of Oscar coming in, because for the first time since they'd met, Oscar seemed to be entirely at ease. He wasn't tense. He wasn't looking around as if expecting someone to hurt him. He was even smiling, and that meant enough to Ignatius that he wouldn't have cared if Oren had kicked his ass out of the team.

"I thought I'd find you asleep," he told Oscar.

Oscar's cheeks reddened. "I was hungry. I wasn't sure I'd find something to eat, but James lives here, too, so there was food in the fridge."

"That's good." Oscar needed more food than what his father had allowed him to eat. "What about your back? Do you need me to ask Fyfe if there's a healer in the coven?"

"I'm fine. The antibiotics you gave me helped a lot. I didn't even have to take the painkillers today." He looked around, and while he was still relaxed, Ignatius could see how overwhelmed he was. His eyes were glazed over, and he looked tired. He could probably use the sleep, and honestly, so could Ignatius. He hadn't slept deeply last night, too worried about Oscar and what was happening with his father. He'd been right when he'd thought Becket wouldn't be able to find them, but that didn't mean he hadn't worried over it.

He pushed himself up from the bed. It was harder than it ought to be, as if the tiredness had hit him at once. "I'll let you rest, then."

"Wait."

Ignatius froze. "Yes?"

Oscar licked his lips. "Are *you* okay?"

Ignatius blinked. "Me?" No one ever asked him if he was okay. He was an old vampire. He was a conclave enforcer. No one ever thought to worry about him, and he'd never cared much about that. But knowing that Oscar wanted to know how he was, to make sure he was all right, was a hit to the heart, and Ignatius wasn't sure how to deal with it.

Oscar smiled. "Yes, you. Unless there's someone else in this room with us?"

"There isn't. Of course. I—I'm fine."

"You don't look fine. Tired."

Ignatius smiled. "I *am* tired. All of this isn't anything new for me, but that doesn't mean I don't need a good night's sleep." Although there was a part that was new to him, the one where he cared for one of the people involved much more than he should. That was the more tiring part. He'd been on alert ever since he'd first met Oscar, because he didn't want to miss anything that might hurt him. He'd managed, but now he felt like he could sleep for a day.

"We both need some sleep."

"We do. And while this room is comfortable, feel free to knock on my door if you need anything. I'm right next door, on your left. Don't worry about disturbing me, because that won't be a problem."

Ignatius moved toward the door, but Oscar stopped him again.

"I don't want to be alone," he said, his voice small in a way Ignatius never wanted to hear again. It was as if Oscar expected him to get angry at the way he was feeling, maybe even to hit him. It wasn't surprising considering the way Oscar's father had treated him, but Ignatius wanted Oscar to know he'd never raise a hand on him, not even if he was angry — and he wasn't.

Ignatius cleared his throat. "Do you want me to call James?" Fyfe would probably try to kick Ignatius' ass if he did that, but he'd understand.

"No. He's my friend, but I can't imagine the two of us spending the night together, and I don't want to take him away from Fyfe."

"Fyfe is no doubt relieved to have him back." Even though James hadn't been away from his new lover for long, Ignatius knew Fyfe well enough to be sure that he'd freaked out — before he started making his calls both to Ignatius and one of the conclave members, Maurice.

Oscar smiled bemusedly. "I can't say I thought James would manage to find himself a man while he was on the run, and a vampire at that. I can't imagine how they met."

"You didn't ask Fyfe?"

"I didn't want to stick my nose where it didn't belong. Besides, James is my friend, but I don't know Fyfe, even though he doesn't seem to have a problem sharing personal details about their life together."

Ignatius chuckled. "That's Fyfe for you. Just tell him to fuck off if you don't want details about what he and James do in their bedroom. He won't mind."

Oscar nodded. "I will. You sound like you know him well."

"I do." Ignatius eyed the bed. "You said you didn't want to be alone tonight?"

"I'd like you to stay, if that's okay with you. I don't expect anything, of course, and I'll understand if you say no, but I've never spent a night not in my bed in my entire life other than yesterday. That and everything else, well, it's overwhelming, and you're the only person I know here apart from James."

Ignatius didn't want to do this, yet he wanted to. He could tell Oscar only wanted some company, and it made sense. His life had been turned upside down, and he probably felt alone in the world right now. He was latching onto Ignatius because he knew him, even if only a little. "You're safe here."

"I know I am. I still don't want to be alone. Please? I want to share a bed, nothing more. I wouldn't presume—"

"All right." He *could* presume, and he'd be right. Ignatius wasn't about to say that out loud, though. Oscar was in a new place, surrounded by new people, and he wouldn't go back to his old life. Ignatius wasn't going to take advantage of him, no matter how much his dick wanted him to. He'd learned a long time ago to ignore that part of himself when it tried to make the decisions for him, and this was no different, even though he could admit, at least to himself, that it wasn't merely physical. "Why don't you get into bed?" he suggested. "I'm going to grab a shower in my room, but I'll be back as soon as I'm done. You should try to relax. Maybe watch TV? I'm sure you can find something."

Ignatius left without giving Oscar time to answer. He hoped Oscar would be asleep by the time he came back. He loved talking to Oscar, but this would be too much. Sharing a bed, being so close while being relaxed, all of that could lead to mistakes made, and it wasn't something Ignatius could allow. He couldn't make mistakes when it came to Oscar.

But of course, Oscar was still awake when Ignatius slunk back into his bedroom fifteen minutes later. He sat up when he heard the door, and the blankets pooled around his waist. He was wearing a t-shirt, but the collar was large enough that it exposed Oscar's collarbones—and Ignatius wanted to follow those lines with his lips, dammit.

"You said you and Fyfe were friends?" Oscar asked as Ignatius slipped into bed.

Ignatius stayed on his side, as close to the edge of the mattress as he dared while hoping he wouldn't end the day flat on his face on the carpet. "We are. We've known each other a while."

"How much is a while? I know that for you vampires, it doesn't mean the same thing as it does for me."

"I don't know exactly. We tend to lose track of things after a while. But at least a couple of hundred years."

"Wow. That's a long time." Oscar wiggled, and he slid closer to the middle of the bed—closer to Ignatius.

"It is. But we haven't talked in a while. Vampires tend to drift apart after a while. It's not like the relationships you have that last twenty, thirty years. We can be together a lot longer than that, and it sometimes makes things complicated."

Oscar rolled to his side and propped himself up on his elbow. He was right next to Ignatius now, so close that Ignatius could feel his warm breath on his skin. "So you two were together? Like, a couple?"

"For a while. We're only friends now, though, and I think we work better that way. Besides, Fyfe has James now." Fyfe was protective, and he liked having someone to take care of. James was perfect for him, while Ignatius had been too independent. He'd wanted to take care of Fyfe as much as Fyfe had wanted to take care of him, and that had made them clash.

"And who do *you* have?"

Well, shit. "My job doesn't leave me a lot of time for personal relationships."

"That's a pity. You deserve love as much as anyone else."

"Not everyone thinks that."

Oscar leaned forward, and, to Ignatius' surprise, pressed a gentle kiss at the corner of Ignatius' lips. It could have led to more, and it would have, had it been anyone else. But Oscar just kissed Ignatius and settled into bed, close enough that if he rolled over, he'd end up in Ignatius' arms.

It took a long time for Ignatius to fall asleep.

CHAPTER FIVE

"Oren wants to talk to you," Ignatius said.

Oscar scowled at the ceiling. "Why? I already told him everything I knew." And he didn't want to know what had happened to his father. He knew that Oren and the rest of Ignatius' team had gone to the pack and had closed the investigation, and that could only mean that his father wasn't in the picture anymore.

He wasn't sure how to feel about that.

He'd never loved his father. He couldn't even call the man a father, because he hadn't been one. He might have provided Oscar with a roof over his head and some food, although never enough for him to feel truly satiated, but he'd been cruel and hateful, and Oscar doubted he'd loved him, just like Oscar hadn't loved his father. But knowing he was dead felt weird, like the last tether to Oscar's old life was gone and he could now start a new life.

He had no idea where to start.

He'd been with the coven — and Ignatius — for a week, and no one expected him to know what he wanted from life. Fyfe had been clear when he'd introduced Oscar to the coven. He was now a coven member, and while he'd gotten some of that cold shoulder he'd expected, he'd also felt incredibly welcomed by some of the vampires he shared the house with. Most of them didn't care that he was a werewolf. They cared that he was a person, and they wanted to get to know him. Oscar was glad, and for the first time in his life, he felt like things would be okay, but it was overwhelming, and he spent a lot of time in his bedroom alone to recuperate. He'd never been a social person, maybe because he hadn't been allowed to, or maybe because it just wasn't him, and he was finding it hard to suddenly share his living space with a bunch of other people.

Ignatius sat on the bed next to Oscar. "He hasn't told me."

Oscar rolled his eyes. "I don't believe that."

It got a smile out of Ignatius. "All right, I confess. He did hint, and I'd like to come with you if you don't mind. But I think he should be the one to tell you."

"I already know my father's dead."

He half expected Ignatius to say he wasn't, but he didn't. "You're right. He is. I'm not sorry."

Oscar barked out a laugh. "I doubt anyone is." He pushed himself into a sitting position. "All right. Where's Oren?" The sooner Oscar talked to him, the sooner he could come back to his room. He realized he should probably make more of an effort to mingle, but he'd just spent part of the night watching TV with Andrew and Falkner. He liked them, even though he'd felt like a third wheel most of the movie, but he was ready for some quiet.

Quiet he wouldn't get, apparently.

"He's with Fyfe in his office."

"Let's go." Oscar slid off the bed and headed toward the bedroom door, but Ignatius caught his arm and pulled him close. Oscar went, more than willing to have Ignatius' attention on him.

The past week had been weird for them. Oscar had no idea what they were doing, but he liked sleeping next to Ignatius — they'd shared a bed every day since they'd arrived — and waking up in his arms. It made him feel cherished, and the only thing that would be better was if Ignatius wanted more. Oscar wasn't sure he didn't, but Ignatius was incredibly cautious with him, too much so maybe. Oscar wanted him, but he was afraid to ask, especially now that Ignatius' team was back and he'd have to go back to work. Oscar wasn't sure how the enforcers worked, but he doubted Ignatius would be able to stick around much longer, and he wasn't about to ask him to. He wouldn't be the reason Ignatius renounced a job he did to help people.

"I'm here for you," Ignatius murmured.

Oscar wrapped his arms around Ignatius' waist and pressed his cheek against Ignatius' chest. He sighed deeply, inhaling Ignatius' scent and relaxing. "I know."

"Whatever happens, whatever Oren asks of you, I'm not going anywhere."

Oscar tilted his head up. "So you already know he's going to ask something from me."

Ignatius grimaced. "I suspect he will. I'm not sure, because he hasn't told me, but yeah."

Oscar hesitated, but he needed to know. "Are you going back to work now that your team is back?"

"Not for a bit. Don't worry about that, Oscar. You'll be the first to know when that happens. I still have some things to take care of, though." He smiled. "Someone to take care of."

Oscar should probably have minded, but he didn't. He *liked* having someone taking care of him, especially if it was Ignatius.

Fyfe and Oren were talking when Oscar and Ignatius got to Fyfe's office. James was there, too, and he looked angry, much more than Oscar had seen him since he'd been jailed by his father.

"What happened?" he asked. Had his father escaped or something? Ignatius had said he'd died, but Oscar had gotten to the point that he thought anything could happen.

"Why don't you sit down?" Fyfe suggested.

"Spit it out. What happened?" Oscar asked, but he obeyed, pulling Ignatius along to one of the empty chairs. Ignatius sat, and Oscar snuggled in his lap, needing the support. He didn't care that it might look weird, or that Oren's eyebrows shot up his forehead when he saw them. He needed Ignatius.

Oren cleared his throat. "As I'm sure Ignatius already told you, your father is dead. The conclave carried out the execution a few days ago. He was recognized guilty of plotting against his alpha, Alpha Torres, and of killing him."

"That's good." Oscar didn't care that everyone still seemed more than happy to ignore his abuse. His father was dead, and that was what counted.

His father wouldn't hurt anyone ever again. *That* was the important thing.

"It is. It also means that since your father hadn't yet appointed a beta, you're the one in charge of the pack right now."

Oren didn't pull punches, did he? And this one hit Oscar right in the solar plexus. His breath hitched, and he leaned against Ignatius' chest. "Me."

Oren nodded. "Yes. I know this isn't what you wanted to hear, but it's a fact. The pack doesn't have a leader right now, because you're here."

"I don't want any of that. I don't want to be their alpha. I don't even want to go back."

"I know. You're going to have to, though."

Oscar couldn't deal with this. He couldn't have the weight of the entire pack on his shoulders, not when he knew he was going to stumble, make a mistake, and disappoint everyone. He wasn't made to be the leader of anything, but especially not of the pack who'd sat back and watched while his father whipped him.

His back twinged with the memory, and he tried to push himself even closer to Ignatius. Ignatius cupped the back of Oscar's neck with a hand and rubbed his thumb against the skin there. "Relax, Oscar. I told you I'd be there for you, whatever happens."

"I don't want to be an alpha. I *can't* be one."

"Then don't be," Fyfe piped up. "No one said you had to accept that charge. You can go there, nominate someone else as alpha, and come back. This is your home now. We'll be waiting for you, and if you want, I can send someone with you, although I can't say how your fellow werewolves will take their presence."

"I'll go with him," Ignatius said with a growl in his voice.

Fyfe wasn't impressed. He flashed Ignatius a wide, wicked grin. "I had no doubt you would. You haven't let him out of your sight since the two of you arrived here."

"I'll go, too," Oren said, and *that* surprised Oscar.

"Why?" he asked.

"Because from what I know about the pack members, at least a few of them are going to do anything they can to convince you to choose them, while others will try to convince you to stay and will try to lead through you. I'm not saying you're weak or anything, but—"

"Oh, you can say it, because I know I am. I was never made to be an alpha, and neither was my father. I'm more than happy to select someone else and come home."

"Then Ignatius and I will make sure no one tries to intimidate you, and we'll escort you home once everything is said and done."

The sooner they left, the sooner they'd get to the pack, and the sooner they could come home. Ignatius wasn't sure when he'd started thinking of Fyfe's coven as home, but it had to be over the past week. Mostly, he knew it had to do with Oscar.

Ignatius wanted Oscar to feel comfortable and happy, and that wouldn't happen when they were back with his pack. Oscar might not be a hundred percent okay with living with the coven right now, but he still liked it better than living with the pack, and anyone could see how anxious going back made him, even though it was hopefully only for a short visit.

"Will we get there before the sun hurts the two of you?" Oscar asked from the back seat of Oren's SUV. He and Ignatius were both sitting there, even though it might seem weird to leave the front seat next to Oren empty. Oscar needed Ignatius, and Ignatius didn't want to leave him alone, even if it was only in the back seat of a car.

"The windows are tinted, but yes, we should manage, Oren answered.

"Where will we be staying?"

"I think your father's house is probably the easiest option for us. You need to stay with the pack until you make a decision. They wouldn't like it if you didn't, and I suspect they'd use that as a reason to ignore you."

Oscar scoffed. "And how is that a bad thing?"

Ignatius and Oren exchanged a glance in the rearview mirror. Ignatius nodded and turned to Oscar. "I know you don't like the pack and the people who form it."

"You're right. I don't."

"They were victims of your father. Even when he was only the beta, they had to obey him."

Oscar's eyes narrowed. "Are you trying to excuse what they did? What they ignored?"

"No. If I could kill your father again, I'd do it, and gladly. And you're right. The pack members should have gone to Alpha Torres to tell him what your father was doing if he didn't already know. I never knew the man, but he didn't strike me as a good alpha, not from what I know about him. He wasn't cruel like your father, and he tried, but he was blind to a lot of things, including what your father was doing to you. The man should never have become the beta, and now you're left with his mess. But, Oscar, remember how scared you were?

How terrified of your father you felt? You didn't go to Alpha Torres even after you heard your father plan his murder."

"I know I was wrong."

"You're right, you were, but it's understandable. You knew what would happen to you if your father found out. Hell, he beat you just because you heard the conversation. Sometimes, fear makes us cowards, and that's okay. It's human nature, and nothing you can change most of the time. *You* did change, though, and I think you should give the people still in the pack a chance to do the same."

Oscar's cheeks were flushed. "I didn't change," he muttered.

Ignatius grabbed his hand and kissed the back of it. "You did. You knew what would happen if you freed James, yet you did."

"I couldn't let him die. I'd already let Alpha Torres die, and I wasn't going to let it happen again."

"You had more courage than a lot of people. But even though the people in the pack didn't have that courage, they don't deserve to be abandoned. They don't deserve to have another alpha like your father, and you know that only the strongest and probably worst of the pack members will try to take your father's place. As much as you hate going back, there's a reason you're doing it. You want to do the right thing."

Oscar sighed, and the tension left him. "Yeah, I do. I might hate the bunch of them, but you're right. They don't deserve to go through this again. I don't think I could forgive myself if I let that happen."

Ignatius smiled. "I know." That was one of the things he loved about Oscar. He wanted to do the right thing, even when it was hard, even when it hurt.

"Do you have an idea about who would make a good alpha?" Oren asked.

Oscar sighed and leaned against Ignatius' side. "I'm not sure. There are a few people who don't completely suck, but I have no idea if they'd be good leaders, or how they'd hold up under pressure. My father wasn't very keen on letting me mingle, probably because he was afraid Alpha Torres would either find out what he was doing to me or that he wouldn't be able to continue ignoring it if he already knew. Besides, my father didn't want to give me a chance to run. I can't say I wouldn't have if I'd had the chance, especially at the end."

"But you've lived there all your life. You have to have at least an idea."

Ignatius could see Oscar didn't want to say it. He wasn't sure why, but he respected that. Still, he and Oren were there because they wanted to help, and they couldn't if Oscar didn't tell them what was going on. "I'd say your father's friends are out."

Oscar snorted. "They are. They're just like him, and they'd treat the pack members like slaves."

"Maybe someone from Alpha Torres' entourage?"

Oscar frowned. "Maybe."

"You're thinking about someone in particular, aren't you?"

Oscar blinked. "How do you know?"

"I can see it."

"You think you know me that well already? It's only been a little over a week since we met."

Ignatius knew Oscar was right. He squeezed Oscar's hand. "I was trained to read people, remember?" he said to avoid talking about why he knew what Oscar was thinking about. He'd spent so much time staring at Oscar, observing him and trying to understand him, that he felt he did know him. And maybe he wasn't wrong. "Who is it?"

Oscar leaned back against the seat. "He's a pack member, but he travels a lot for work."

"Who, Oscar?"

"Alpha Torres' brother."

Ignatius knew about the man, of course. He and the rest of the team had studied Alpha Torres, his life and his family, especially once they'd realized James had nothing to do with his death and that they were only trying to catch him because they'd been ordered to. On paper, the man didn't sound like a bad choice, but being the alpha's brother didn't mean he would be a good alpha. Of course, it would be near impossible to do worse than Becket had been, so there was that, and since Oscar wanted to go home as soon as possible, Ignatius wasn't going to linger to make sure the guy was perfect for the job. No one was perfect, not even Fyfe, and he was a damn good coven leader. He was kind of forceful, though, and he sometimes took advantage of the fact that he was their leader to impose things, like he had in James' case. The main reason the coven had accepted James initially was that Fyfe had wanted him there. That had changed now that they were getting to know him, but it didn't change that fact.

"You think he'll want to take his brother's place?" Oren asked.

"Maybe? I honestly have no idea. I think they were close, and I know for sure that he was pissed with my father when he came home for Alpha Torres' funeral, but my father had his posse, and they forced him out, although I think that having to travel for his job also helped with that."

"Was he home when I was there?" Ignatius asked.

"I don't know. I told you, he doesn't come around often."

"Do you know how to contact him?"

"No, but we could look through Alpha Torres' stuff. My father had everything boxed up when he died. I'm not sure where it is, but probably at his house. I don't think his brother went there after he died. He left fast after the funeral. Maybe his wife could do it? With him as her beta?"

They didn't have much to go on, but it was a start, and it

was better than what Ignatius had imagined. Now they just had to find a way to contact Alpha Torres' brother and convince him to become the next alpha.

Piece of cake, right?

Oscar was *not* looking forward to this. He could feel himself tense up more and more as the panorama outside the window changed into something vaguely familiar. He didn't want to go back. He hadn't thought he ever would. Even though Ignatius had tried to mention the fact that once his father died, Oscar would be the one in charge, Oscar had done his best to ignore it. He didn't want to be an alpha. He'd be terrible at it. He could barely make decisions for himself on the best of days, so there was no way he could do it on a day-to-day basis for an entire pack.

"We're here," Oren said, even though he didn't need to. Oscar could see where they were, and he didn't want to be there.

It helped that Ignatius was still holding his hand, though. He hadn't let go since he'd first grabbed it at the beginning of their drive. Oren had probably broken a few speeding laws to get them there so fast, but Oscar didn't mind. If he had to be there — and he did — he wanted to be gone as soon as possible. He didn't expect the pack's reaction to having him there again would be a good one, and he was right, at least in part.

When Oren parked the car in front of the house where Oscar had spent almost his entire life, there were already two men waiting for them on the porch. Oscar didn't need to see them from up close to know who they were. His father had many friends, but those two were the closest to him, and they were too much like him for Oscar to ever be comfortable with their presence.

"We're already in trouble, I see," Oren said. He didn't

sound worried, and Oscar tried to relax.

He wasn't alone anymore. He had Ignatius and Oren, and they were conclave enforcers. They could beat Billy and Geoff's asses without breaking a sweat, and it would probably be enough for everyone else to keep their distance.

"You kidnapped the kid," Billy said as soon as the SUVs door were open.

Oscar hadn't even had the time to slide out of it, dammit. He stayed back and let Oren and Ignatius handle this. He'd confirm no one had kidnapped him if he needed to, although he was pretty sure no one there believed he had been. Billy and Geoff needed to put up a show where Oscar was the vulnerable, unsure boy who needed them to help him rule the pack. There was no way he'd choose either of them to take his father's place, and they knew it. The only way they could rule over the pack was through him.

Ignatius was right.

"I didn't kidnap him. I saved him from an abusive father who thought nothing of whipping him," Ignatius said. He crossed his arms over his shoulders and stood tall, in front of Oscar, shielding him.

"Oscar's father was trying to discipline him. He thought he was doing the right thing."

"He *knew* he was doing the wrong thing. He knew James Beltran had nothing to do with Alpha Torres' death, yet he put him in jail and would have gotten him killed if Oscar hadn't freed him. He whipped his only son because Oscar did the right thing. That's not a father trying to teach their son. That's an abuser, and he was doing the same thing to the rest of the pack. You still think he was doing the right thing?"

Geoff licked his lips. "He could be a little hard sometimes."

"*Hard*? *Sometimes*?" Oscar asked.

He wasn't afraid of Billy and Geoff anymore. He didn't have to be. He had Ignatius and Oren, and they'd protect him.

Billy bristled. "He did the best he could without your mother. You can't blame him for not liking that James fellow, not when he was a bitten wolf."

"What James is or isn't doesn't change the fact that my father was wrong, or that he was a cruel man."

"He wasn't always like that, and you weren't an easy child. Are you going to make him proud, or are you going to run away like you already did once? You weren't even there when he died." He cast a disgusted glance toward Oren, letting all of them know exactly what he thought of his decision.

"Make him proud?" Oscar couldn't think of a worse thing than his father being proud of him. It would mean he'd gone down the same alley his father had followed, and that wasn't something he wanted to happen. He'd rather die than become a man similar to his father.

Geoff nodded and stepped forward. "I could be your beta. Me or Billy. We can help you navigate this and become a good alpha."

Oscar's skin crawled. They thought he was going to say *yes,* didn't they? Or maybe they thought they could manipulate him into saying *yes* or force him. He had no doubt they would have done just that if he'd come alone, or if he'd still been with the pack when Oren had sentenced his father to death.

Oscar was the one with the power right now. He was the one who was technically the alpha. He was the one who made the rules, and who would pick a beta. That was, if he wanted to be the alpha. As it was, he couldn't think of a worse thing to do with his life. And even if he *had* decided to accept the job, Billy and Geoff would both make for horrible betas. They were made of the same cloth his father had been made with — greedy, cruel, people who wanted power to benefit them and not because they could do something good with it. Oscar wouldn't choose them even if they tried to pay him for it.

"The two of you should leave," Oren said.

Geoff glared. "We want to know what Oscar is planning to do. It's our right to know. We live here. This is our pack."

"And for now, he's your alpha, and he wants you to leave."

"That's not what he said," Billy piped up. He narrowed his eyes at Oscar.

Even though Oscar knew he had nothing to fear, he couldn't help but feel suddenly cold.

Oren looked at Oscar. "Oscar?"

Ignatius was still there, still shielding Oscar with his body, and that was the only reason Oscar managed to push out the words. "Yes. I want you to leave."

"You can't—"

"He can do whatever he wants. He's the alpha. And we're here to make sure the entire pack, including you, knows it. It's late, and we all need to sleep. You'd better go."

"It's late for you, bloodsucker, not for us."

"Maybe so, but Oscar has gotten used to our timetable, and we just spent the night driving, so either way, he needs sleep. He'll organize a meeting tonight to talk to the pack. In the meantime, you two need to leave and go to work, or whatever it is you do during the day."

Oscar could tell his father's friends weren't happy with being ordered around by a vampire, but they didn't say anything. Oren could decide he didn't like the way they talked to him and execute them for it. The conclave and its enforcers were supposed to uphold the laws, but that didn't mean some of them didn't abuse them and use them the way they wanted.

Billy and Geoff weren't happy, but they did obey, and Oscar relaxed. He let Ignatius steer him toward the house, even though the last thing he wanted right now was to walk into the place that had been his prison for so long. He had to, though. This was the most logical place for them to spend the night. He hoped it would only be one night, but he knew better than to let himself hope. But even if it wasn't, he'd be out of there soon enough, and that was what counted.

Oscar wasn't staying, and once he left, he wouldn't come back, not this time, not for anything in the world.

"That was intense," Ignatius said after he closed the front door behind them.

"They're like my father. I should have expected them to be here. How did they even find out we were coming?"

"They suspected you'd come back. You had to. I bet they kept an eye out for any car they didn't recognize and rushed here as soon as they noticed one."

Oscar sighed and rubbed his face. "Are we going to bed?"

Oren cleared his throat. "I thought we could talk and maybe try to contact Alpha Torres' brother. The wolves are just getting up and going to work, so we should take advantage of that. Pack territory will be empty enough for us to manage not to make people realize what we're doing."

Oscar groaned. He should have known things weren't going to be easy.

Ignatius wanted to bundle Oscar up and drag him to his old bedroom to sleep, but Oren was right. It was early morning, possibly the best moment for them to talk to whoever Oscar thought would be a good alpha. Most of the pack would be leaving for work soon if they hadn't already, and while Oscar seemed to be ready for sleep, it would need to wait an hour or two.

"How do we contact Alpha Torres' brother?" he asked.

"I don't have his phone number. He lives in the house next to Alpha Torres', but I'm not even sure he's here right now. I told you, he travels a lot for work. You should be able to find his wife, though."

That might mean the man couldn't be the alpha. Alphas

needed to stick close to the pack. It didn't mean they couldn't work, although not all of them did, but they did have to be present in case something happened and to deal with every-day problems.

Oren nodded. "I'm going to run over there and see if I can find him. You and Ignatius should use that time to freshen up, and maybe you could eat. I'll be back as soon as possible."

Oscar opened his mouth, but he snapped it shut and nodded. "All right."

Ignatius waited until Oren was gone to take Oscar's hand. "Everything okay?"

Oscar closed his eyes and shrugged. "I don't know. I don't like being here, even though I realize why it's so important. I still wish I could have stayed home in my bed, though."

Knowing that Oscar already considered the coven his home made Ignatius smile. "I think the three of us wish that."

Oscar opened his eyes. "You're right. I might hate being here, but I'm not the only one, yet you two haven't been whin-ing about it. I should stop."

"Maybe, but not for me. I don't care how much you com-plain about things. You can talk to me about everything and whine for as long as you need to feel better."

"I don't know what I did to deserve you." Oscar's cheeks flushed. "You know, as a friend."

Ignatius didn't think holding hands like they'd been doing almost constantly since they'd left the coven meant they were friends, but this probably wasn't the right moment to tell Os-car he was falling stupidly in love with him, so Ignatius just squeezed Oscar's hand and kissed the back of it. "Do you want to go to the kitchen to find something to eat?"

"No, but let's go."

Ignatius wasn't surprised to find things he had to throw away in the fridge, although it wasn't much. It looked like no one had come around to clean the house since Becket had died, which was both understandable and surprising. "Sit down. I'll make you a sandwich."

"You shouldn't have to. I can do it."

Ignatius frowned as he took out the bread after opening two different cupboards looking for it. "I know I don't have to. I *want* to make it for you."

"Why? You don't even eat."

"So? You're my friend. I like taking care of you."

"You do?"

Ignatius understood why Oscar sounded so surprised, but he hated it. "I like you, Oscar. I know we started as conclave enforcer and witness, but we left that behind almost right away. I thought you'd realized that, too."

"I did. It's just . . . I don't know. I'm not exactly sure why you want to be my friend." He wasn't looking at Ignatius, and Ignatius didn't like it.

"Because you're a sweet, good man who's been given a lot of hate in life and who didn't deserve it. No one deserves to go through what you went through, and surprisingly, you came out of it still a good man. You should have someone to take care of you and show you how nice it can be. You should have someone who wants the best for you."

"And that's you? You're that person?"

"I think I am." He hoped he was.

The front door opening cut their conversation short, but Ignatius made a mental note to bring this up again later. He wanted Oscar to understand that he wasn't going anywhere and that he'd be there for him, whatever happened. He didn't expect anything in return, didn't *want* anything in return. He'd be happy just making *Oscar* happy, and that by itself told him how important Oscar had become to him.

"They're in the kitchen," he heard Oren say, and to his surprise, when Oren walked into the kitchen, he was followed by a woman rather than the man they expected.

Oscar blinked at her. "I wasn't expecting this."

The woman gave him a cautious smile. "My husband is away for work right now."

Oscar cocked his head. "You know, this might not be a bad idea."

The woman's eyes widened. "What are you talking about?"

Ignatius placed the plate with the sandwich he'd prepared for Oscar on the table in front of him, wiped his hands, and offered one to the woman. "I'm Ignatius."

She shook it. "I'm Maria. Alpha Torres was my brother-in-law."

"Why don't we all sit down?" Oren suggested.

Maria looked uncomfortable, but she sat in one of the chairs, her back straight, her gaze on Oscar. She licked her lips. "What can I do for you, Alpha?"

Oscar grimaced. "God, no. Please don't call me that."

"I'm sorry. What should I call you?"

"Oscar is fine, although I won't be here long, so whatever."

"I don't understand why I'm here."

Oscar put down his sandwich. "I don't want to be the alpha. I'd be a terrible alpha, to be honest. The only reason I'm here is that my father never chose a beta, so the pack falls to me. I'm going to choose someone I think will be better at this than my father and me, although I'll admit that's not going to be hard."

Maria's eyes widened. "And you thought my husband would be a good alpha?"

"I did, although I never got to know him well. As you said, he's often away for work, and now that I think about it, that probably disqualifies him from becoming alpha. You, on the other hand, work in town, right?"

"I don't—I can't."

Ignatius didn't ask the questions that were burning to

come out. He'd have time later. He trusted Oscar, so if Oscar thought Maria would be the best alpha, he was all for it.

"Why not?" Oscar asked.

"I'm a woman."

"Who cares? Wait, actually, I do. You're probably going to be the best alpha this pack has ever had. My father only thought about what he could gain from the position, and while Alpha Torres wasn't as bad, well, let's just say I had things to complain about when he was alpha. But I've seen you with your children, and I suspect you'd treat the pack members in pretty much the same way."

"I'm only a mother."

Oscar leaned forward. "A mother who's been raising her three kids almost alone, since your husband is away a lot. Look, the pack needs a change. It's obvious that men almost ruined everything, and I put myself into that group. There are things I could and should have done differently, but I can't change the past. I *can* change the future, though, and I'm going to do my best for that to happen. I'd like you to be the next alpha. If you say yes, we'll announce it tonight, and I'll be home by tomorrow morning."

Maria cocked her head. "Home?"

Oscar smiled at Ignatius, and if Ignatius hadn't already been in love with him, he'd have fallen right then. "Yeah. I found a place I could call home, even though it's the last thing I expected." He looked back at Maria. "The pack holds a lot of bad memories for me. I don't ever want to come back, and knowing you're the one in charge would help me feel better. You can rebuild the pack, leave the fear my father created behind, and look at the future. I know Alpha Torres would want that. You might not be his brother, but you're his brother's wife, and I know he respected you and loved you. Honestly, I can't think of anyone better."

Oscar snorted. "Billy and Geoff already tried to convince

me to make them betas, and you know what will happen if either of them has even a tiny amount of power here. I might not want to stick around, but that doesn't mean I want the pack to die out."

Ignatius could tell Maria was still hesitant, but he hoped she'd get over it. Like Oscar had said, he wanted to go home.

CHAPTER SIX

Oscar felt Ignatius move against him and smiled. He had no idea what time it was, but from the light that managed to pass his eyelids, it had to be the middle of the day, maybe afternoon. Way too early for Ignatius to get up, that was for sure.

Oscar wrapped his arm around Ignatius' waist. "Where are you going?" He couldn't believe he was in his childhood bed with the man he was in love with. His younger self would never have believed such a thing was possible, and his adult self still wanted to pinch himself to make sure it wasn't a dream.

"There's someone here."

That got Oscar's full attention. He slid his arm away from Ignatius and tried to sit up, but Ignatius pushed him back down before he could. "Stay," Ignatius murmured.

Oscar nodded. He'd be as useful as a wet noodle if there was a fight, so it would be better for everyone if he stayed out of it. Oren was sleeping downstairs on the couch, and maybe he hadn't heard whatever Ignatius had heard, but Oscar had no doubt that he'd be there as soon as something happened. He could help Ignatius much better than Oscar could even dream of.

Ignatius slid off the bed, and now that Oscar knew what he was looking for, he couldn't help but notice the shadow at the window. There was someone on the roof trying to open the window.

The window clicked and moved upward, and two hands

then a head appeared. Oscar didn't have enough time to see what was happening or who it was, because Ignatius grabbed the head and pulled it inside as if the person it belonged to weighed nothing. The person — a man from the voice — yelped and stumbled inside. Ignatius pushed the man to the floor, twisting his arms behind him, and sat on his back.

"What do you want?" he asked with a growl that made Oscar shiver.

Oscar sat up and peeked over the edge of the mattress. He realized that Ignatius was sitting on Billy's back, but then he got distracted by the fact that part of Ignatius' body was in the sun and that his skin was getting red — too red not to hurt. Ignatius didn't even seem to have noticed, but Oscar jumped out of bed. "You need to move away from the window," he said, pushing the curtains closed. They didn't entirely cut the light, but it was enough to shield Ignatius from the direct sunlight.

"I'm fine." Ignatius used his hold on Billy to slam his chest to the floor. "What are you doing here?" he asked again.

Oscar knew better than to try to baby Ignatius. He'd have to wait until Billy had been dealt with, whatever that entailed.

The door flew open. "What's going on?"

Oren stood there, bare-chested, ready to strike. He relaxed when he saw Ignatius and Billy and stepped in, and Oscar realized his feet were bare, too. It made him look vulnerable yet not, and Oscar had never seen him that way. Of course, he wasn't exactly close to Oren.

"He won't tell me why he's here," Ignatius said.

"That might because you're still slamming him to the floor and he can't answer. Come on. Hand him over. I'll take care of this, and you should take care of that burn on your arm."

"I'm fine," Ignatius said, but he did get up. He hauled Billy to his feet and pushed him toward Oren, who caught him as if he weighed nothing. What was it with those guys? Oscar would have fallen along with Billy if he'd had to hold him up, yet there Ignatius and Oren were, handling him easily.

"I didn't do anything," Billy said, and he sounded out of breath. Maybe the reason he hadn't answered before really was that he couldn't.

"You broke into the house through the window. That's not nothing," Oren said. He was holding the back of Billy's shirt, and he gave him a good shake that made Billy's teeth rattle.

"I just wanted to talk to Oscar without you two around! How was I supposed to know he was fucking a vampire?"

Oscar's cheeks heated, but he didn't look away. He wasn't fucking Ignatius, but it was in his plans if he managed to convince Ignatius, and he wasn't ashamed. He loved Ignatius. His father would have laughed in his face if he'd ever told him something like that, and Oscar supposed a lot of people would think it was too soon, since they'd only met a little over a week ago, but Oscar knew that was what he felt. He might not have any experience when it came to relationships, but that didn't mean he'd never loved.

"Shut it," Ignatius snapped.

Oren gave Billy another shake. "What Oscar does or doesn't do and who he does it with is none of your concern." He started dragging Billy toward the hallway. "I'll take care of him. Don't worry."

"What does that mean?" Billy asked with a squeak.

"You're about to find out."

Ignatius slammed the door closed behind them and leaned against it.

"What did Oren mean?" Oscar asked. He didn't care about Billy, but he didn't want anyone to die just because they tried to sneak in through his window.

"He'll probably tie him up and dump him somewhere until this evening. Don't worry. He won't hurt him much, just slam him around a bit and try to find out why he was here, although I suppose that's easy enough to understand."

"He wanted to try to intimidate me."

"Possibly. He wanted to become your beta. He thinks he'll be able to manipulate you."

And he probably would have managed if Oscar hadn't met Ignatius. He'd have been entirely alone to face this after his father had died, and he was in no way ready for that even now that he had Ignatius, James, and Fyfe, and hell, even Oren. "Thank you," he murmured.

Ignatius' arm caught Oscar's gaze again, and Oscar rushed to the bathroom. He'd always stocked up on bandages and whatnot because he needed them when his father beat him, so he had more than enough stuff to take care of Ignatius. "Sit on the bed," he said when he walked back into the bedroom.

He expected Ignatius to argue that it was nothing, but to his surprise, Ignatius obeyed. He settled on the edge of the mattress, and Oscar kneeled next to him. He didn't usually deal with burns, but he made do, and Ignatius didn't protest. "I can't believe you got hurt protecting me. I hate it."

Ignatius gently touched Oscar's hair. "What else could I have done? I don't want you to get hurt, ever."

"I know. Just like I don't want you to get hurt. I still don't like the idea, though." He stroked his fingertips along Ignatius' arm and sighed. "I'm sorry. I know it's your job, and I know you wanted to protect me, but I still don't like it."

"It's okay."

Oscar looked up. He licked his lips, his mind suddenly blank. He and Ignatius had shared a bed since that first night with the coven, but that was the only time in the day they were that close, and they were asleep for most of it. As soon as he woke up, Ignatius always fled the bed, as if he didn't want Oscar to catch him wrapped around him.

Oscar wanted nothing more than to wake up like that. He wanted more than what they had. He wanted the nights to be full of them, of Ignatius, not only the days, when he couldn't even feel it.

He swallowed and leaned forward, closer to Ignatius. Ignatius frowned, but before he could say anything, Oscar kissed him.

He didn't know if he was a good kisser, but he doubted it, since this was his first kiss. Since he didn't want to make a mess, he limited himself to pressing his lips against Ignatius' a few times.

Then Ignatius gently pushed him away.

Oscar's cheeks felt like they were on fire. He jerked away and rose to his feet, grabbing the supplies he'd used. He needed to get them back to the bathroom—where he could deal with his shame on his own—but Ignatius grabbed his wrist to stop him. "Oscar."

"What?" Oscar's voice was too harsh, and his heart was racing.

"Why did you kiss me?"

That wasn't what Oscar had expected. "Because I wanted to."

"Not because it was an easy way for you to thank me? Or because you're grateful I took care of Billy?"

Oscar blinked. "Easy? You think that was easy for me to do?"

"Oscar. Answer the question. Did you kiss me because you're grateful, or is it more?"

"It's more, you idiot. Haven't you noticed how I feel about you?"

Oscar wanted to explain himself, to yell at Ignatius and then go hide in the bathroom and try to start getting over his heartache, but Ignatius pulled him closer, cupped his cheek with his free hand, and kissed him again.

Ignatius hoped he wasn't making a massive mistake by kissing Oscar, but he couldn't resist any longer, not when Oscar had kissed him first. How was he supposed to push him away when this was what he'd wanted from almost the first moment he'd seen him in this very bedroom?

He kept things light and easy because he knew how little experience Oscar had when it came to this and because he wanted to savor their first kiss. He hoped it would be the first of a long line, but he couldn't be sure of that, and he wanted to remember it for as long as he could.

Oscar seemed to have other ideas, though. He dropped the stuff he'd been holding on the floor and scrambled to sit in Ignatius' lap, straddling his thighs. They were both wearing pajama pants, and the thin fabric couldn't hide that Oscar was already hard. It made Ignatius smile — it had been a while since he'd been as young as Oscar was now, when the slightest rubbing on his dick would make it hard.

"What do you want?" he asked. The last thing he wanted was to hurt Oscar, and that was precisely what would happen if they rushed into things. He doubted Oscar had any lube in his old bedroom, and he hadn't packed any. He couldn't have dreamed that this would happen.

Oscar shook his head. "I don't know."

"Okay. You'll tell me if you're uncomfortable with anything we do?"

"Yeah."

Ignatius had to trust Oscar on that, and he did. He was already getting better at saying what he liked and didn't like, at speaking up, and that wasn't something he'd been allowed to do as he grew up. He was now, and he did it.

Ignatius grabbed Oscar's hips and rolled and pushed them up the bed in one movement. Oscar squeaked and wrapped himself around Ignatius, which was nice, but not what Ignatius wanted, not while they were still wearing their pajamas.

He needed them naked for this, as long as Oscar was comfortable with that.

Ignatius pressed Oscar's back on the mattress and leaned back. "Still okay?" he asked as he took off his t-shirt.

Oscar's gaze moved up and down Ignatius' chest. "More than."

"Will you still be okay if I take your clothes off?"

As an answer, Oscar lifted his hips and pushed his pajama pants down his legs. He wasn't wearing anything under them, and Ignatius almost swallowed his tongue at the sight under him.

Oscar's legs were long, and his skin was sprinkled with blond hair. His cock was long, too, and as flushed as his cheeks and his chest, now that Ignatius could see it, since Oscar had taken off his t-shirt, too. Oscar was all pale skin, blond hair, and red flush, and it was so fucking enticing. Ignatius had been with a lot of people over the hundreds of years he'd been alive, but he honestly couldn't remember the last time he'd wanted someone as much as he did now.

"Now you," Oscar said.

He didn't have to say it twice. Ignatius scrambled to drop his pants, shaking his foot to get them off when they got hooked there, and leaned down to press his body against Oscar's. Oscar whimpered and opened his legs, welcoming Ignatius in a way that touched Ignatius' heart to the core.

Oscar trusted him. He wanted him. He might even love him, and it had been so long since Ignatius had been through this, through the discovery of a new relationship—if that was what they had. Ignatius wasn't sure, and he wasn't going to stop what he was doing to ask.

His cock slotted neatly in the crease between Oscar's thigh and his groin. Ignatius rubbed it there, groaning at the pleasure that sparked in his body. He'd wanted this for what he felt was ages, even though it had only been a week or so.

"That feels so good," Oscar said, clinging to Ignatius' shoulders.

Ignatius wanted Oscar to forget where he was and what was happening outside of the bedroom, outside of the bed. He kissed him and thrust his hips, and while he could have used more pressure, Oscar went wild under him, writhing and pushing up.

Ignatius focused on him. He didn't even care about himself, but watching Oscar experimenting this for the first time was so good. All the shyness and reservations were gone from him, and he was unashamed of what he was feeling. He moaned and moved against Ignatius' body, taking what he needed, and it was incredibly sexy.

Oscar shuddered when he came, crying out against Ignatius' lips. Ignatius held him close, gently biting on Oscar's neck. He didn't expect it when Oscar tilted his head to the side. "You can bite me," he said in a hoarse voice.

Ignatius kissed the spot he'd bitten. "Later."

Oscar was drowsy, and even though he kept reaching for Ignatius' cock, Ignatius ignored it. He rolled until he was on his back with Oscar's head neatly tucked against his chest. Oscar rubbed his fingertips down Ignatius' chest, but he didn't reach under the blanket again. "You didn't come," he said, his voice slightly slurred with sleep and pleasure.

"It doesn't matter."

"Why not? Didn't you like this?"

Ignatius kissed the top of Oscar's head. "I loved it. But it can wait."

"The next time we wake up?"

"The next time, yes. I'm not going anywhere, *amore*. I'll still be here when you wake up, and we can do whatever you want to do."

"What does that mean?"

"What?"

"Amore." Oscar did his best to get the pronunciation right. Ignatius smiled. "It means love."

"So you're Italian?"

"In a way. I was in the Roman military when ancient Rome was a thing. Now go to sleep. You need it."

Oscar drifted off eventually, but Ignatius couldn't seem to calm his thoughts down enough to do the same. He always hated sleeping when it was this light outside, because it kept him up, but that wasn't the problem this time. No, this time, his mind was swirling with questions and doubts, and he had no answers to any of them.

He wanted to see where this thing with Oscar would go, but how could he? Being a conclave enforcer meant that he and the rest of his team were sent off where they were needed, and that could be anywhere in the world for any length of time. There was no way to have a relationship this way, especially not with someone who only had a short lifespan next to Ignatius'.

He needed to talk to Oren. He should be able to tell him what to do, how to deal with this. Maybe he could take a leave of absence, if the conclave was okay with it. He wanted to focus on Oscar for however long they'd have together, but he knew he'd eventually come back to the conclave, if it was still there by then. There was no way to be sure of that. Ignatius knew all too well how fast things could change.

He wanted Oscar. He couldn't deny it, and he didn't want to, and it seemed like Oscar wanted him, too. Ignatius was going to do whatever it took to make things work once he was sure Oscar shared his vision of their future, even if it meant giving up the conclave. He wouldn't be the first one to do that or the last, and he'd had decades to help and do what he thought was right. Maybe it was time for him to take a break and see what else life could offer.

He certainly wanted to. Meeting Oscar felt like a second

chance, a chance to get things right and to make sure Oscar was happy. Everything else could wait — would *have* to wait, because Ignatius was doing this.

"You got everything?" Ignatius asked. He slid a hand around Oscar's waist and kissed his forehead even as he looked around the house.

Oscar loved it. It was as if now that he'd been allowed to once, he couldn't stop touching Oscar. Oscar hadn't expected Ignatius to be this affectionate. He wasn't sure why, but when he thought of vampires, especially those who worked for the conclave, he thought of them as cold and unyielding. Ignatius could undoubtedly be that way, but with Oscar, he wasn't. He was gentle and soft, and Oscar couldn't help but think about how they'd be in five years, in ten, hell, maybe even in twenty. He might be an idiot for hoping they'd be together that long considering everything — he was a werewolf, he'd age while Ignatius wouldn't, he was only twenty-four — but he didn't see why he shouldn't.

"Oscar? Do you have everything?" Ignatius asked again, and Oscar realized he'd been so lost in his thoughts that he hadn't answered. He flushed and nodded. "Yeah. There's not much I want to take with me anyway." He'd limited himself to packing his bedroom. He didn't have much, but he was glad he'd be able to take everything that had belonged to his mom. The new alpha could burn everything else if she wanted or give the house to someone who needed it. Oscar was never coming back.

"As long as you're sure."

"I am." Oscar kissed Ignatius' cheek, still in awe that he could do that. He wasn't sure what he and Ignatius were right now, but he knew what he wanted, and that they probably were going to need to talk as soon as possible. It was obvious that Ignatius wanted to be with him, though, or at least he hoped that was what the touches and kisses meant.

Ignatius smiled. "Then I guess we can go."

Oscar nodded. "Do you think the pack will give Maria problems?" He'd declared her the new alpha as soon as he'd managed, once the sun had been down and most of the pack had come home from work. He'd heard the grumbles, and he'd seen the glares, especially coming from Geoff, and Billy's family, but he couldn't have cared less. The majority of the pack seemed to be *happy* about Maria being their new alpha, and Oscar knew she'd make the right decisions.

It was still going to be a shock for her husband when he came home from wherever he was. When the man had left, his wife stayed home with the kids, even though they were teenagers and they didn't need her to. He was coming home to her being in charge of the entire pack.

Oscar hoped he'd made the right choice, but only the future could tell. He doubted he'd ever check in. He wanted the pack and the pack members to do well, but it wasn't his home anymore. He wasn't even sure it ever had been. He wasn't leaving with fond memories of the place, or the people.

Ignatius sighed. "I don't know. I think every alpha has to face problems sooner or later. She seems like she can handle it, though."

Oscar hoped it was true. "Where's Oren?"

"He dragged Billy home. I doubt the man is going to try anything else after the dressing down Oren is no doubt giving him."

"Do you think he would have hurt me if you hadn't been there?" Oscar had forced himself not to think about that, because he didn't want to obsess over it, but it was a genuine possibility.

"I don't know. I don't think he wanted to hurt you, just convince you to make him beta, or alpha if you weren't going to stay. But he might have gotten angry. Who knows? Either way, you don't have to worry about it." He kissed Oscar, on the mouth this time. "Let's go. I can't wait to be back home."

Oscar wanted to ask where home was for Ignatius, who traveled with only a backpack, but he didn't. They'd have time to talk about the future later.

Ignatius grabbed their bags—the boxes Oscar had filled were already in the SUV—while Oscar looked one last time at the house where he'd grown up. It was his past, while his future was walking out the door . . . and stopping?

Oscar rushed to Ignatius' side. "What's going on?"

He dropped his bag when he saw what Ignatius was looking at. "Who left a *baby* here?"

"I have no idea."

The baby was probably a boy, if the blue of his blanket was an indication of his gender, although Oscar didn't want to assume. He was sleeping, looking like he belonged in the car seat he was in. "That's not good, right?"

Ignatius looked at Oscar. "What's not good? That they left a baby on your porch?"

"No, the car seat. I think I read somewhere that they shouldn't spend too much time in them because of their spine or something."

"I have no idea, Oscar. I can't remember the last time I had anything to do with a baby."

"What do we do with him?"

Ignatius looked around, but Oscar hadn't heard anyone, and he doubted Ignatius would have. Whoever had left the baby there had managed to be quiet and to leave without being noticed, maybe when he and Ignatius had been in the shower together.

That memory sent heat to Oscar's cheeks, but he had other things to focus on, because the baby's eyes had opened, and he was staring at them. "He's awake," Oscar whispered.

"I can see that."

"What do we do?"

"We should take him to Maria. She's the alpha. Whoever left this baby has to be a werewolf."

"Why? Because they left him here? You know anyone can walk in and out of pack territory."

"Maybe, but they knew your father wasn't here anymore. Who in their right mind would leave a baby with your father? I think this baby was left for you." Ignatius arched a brow. "Do you have something to tell me?"

It took Oscar a second to realize what he was saying. "No! Of course not. I've never had, you know, with a woman."

"So the baby isn't yours."

"No. Maybe the person who left him there left a note in the seat or something?"

"We'll have to move the baby to find it, in that case." Ignatius made it sound like it was the worst thing that could happen. Oscar wasn't sure he was wrong. He'd never had to deal with a baby either, but when the baby's face scrunched up and he wailed, Oscar acted on instinct, crouching next to him and reaching out. He fumbled with the car seat buckles, and once he managed to open them, he grabbed the baby as gently as he could and raised him. "He smells okay," he said. He'd been terrified at the thought of having to change the baby's diaper, even with the diaper bag that had been left next to the car seat.

"Thank God." Ignatius leaned closer and took a sniff. Oscar thought it was to make sure the baby didn't need to be changed, but Ignatius' eyes widened, and since it wasn't a reaction a lot of things got out of him, Oscar knew something was wrong.

"Is he sick?" he cuddled the baby against his chest, and to his surprise, the baby whimpered and stopped crying.

"I don't know, but I do know he's a dhampir. Werewolf and vampire, from what I smell."

It was Oscar's turn to be stunned. "Are you sure?"

"Smell him."

Oscar pressed his nose against the baby's head. He smelled of baby, but Ignatius was right. Under that sweet scent, there was wolf—*and* vamp. "Dhampirs are rare, aren't they?"

"Very much so, especially wolf-vampire hybrids. Vampires and werewolves don't tend to mix, let alone breed."

"What do we do?"

"We take him to Maria. This is her pack now. So it might be the baby of a pack member."

It was possible, but considering what the baby was, Oscar doubted they'd find his mother. Dhampirs weren't seen with a good eye in the paranormal community, mostly by the same people who thought vampires and wolves shouldn't mix. But she'd left the baby on Oscar's porch for a reason, even though Oscar couldn't even begin to imagine what that reason was. "Do you think Maria will keep him?" he asked.

Ignatius' expression was severe. "I don't know. I hope so."

But they both knew how unlikely that was.

Ignatius already knew what was going to happen when they got to Maria's house. What new alpha would want a hybrid in their pack? Especially one who'd been abandoned and who was a mix of two species known to hate each other. It was bullshit, but that didn't mean most of the paranormal world didn't believe it. Maria was already going to have to deal with a lot now that she was the alpha. Some people wouldn't be happy she was a woman, or that she wasn't related to Alpha Torres or Becket in any way. Some would try to challenge her right to the position because they thought Oscar didn't have the right to choose her. Some would be jealous because they wanted the position. On top of that, she had to deal with her family and her husband.

There was no way she was going to want to add a hybrid baby to the mix.

Which made Ignatius wonder what was going to happen to the kid. He could tell Oscar wasn't going to be happy with Maria's refusal, but that didn't help them.

"I can't, Oscar," Maria said after Oscar explained what had happened and what the baby was.

Oscar clutched the baby—who had quieted down and was sleeping again—to his chest. "He didn't do anything. He's a *baby*. He can't help what he is."

Maria rubbed her forehead. "I know that, and trust me, I wish I could say yes. Like you said, he's only a baby. But the pack isn't going to accept him, and the last thing I need while I'm still trying to come to terms with this is a dhampir baby. And you *know* some people are going to try to use it against me. I can't give them more ammunition, even though it's tempting to say fuck it and drop everything. I don't want my pack to be broken any more than it already is, Oscar, and that's what will happen if Billy or Geoff get what they want."

"What am I supposed to do with him, then?"

Maria arched a brow. "Why don't you keep him?"

Ignatius had his training to thank for the fact that he didn't groan. He'd known this was coming. He'd seen it in the way Oscar handled the baby and in how protective he already was of him. He loved that Oscar cared so much, but a baby? When they'd just gotten together, and they hadn't yet talked about what they wanted and what kind of future they expected?

Oscar blinked. "Me?"

"He seems to like you, and from the way you're holding him, I can tell you're comfortable."

"I am, but that doesn't mean I want to be a dad. I'm only twenty-four."

"I was twenty-two when I had my first kid. But if you don't want to keep him, maybe the conclave could take care of him?"

Oscar and Maria both looked at Ignatius. Ignatius sighed. "The conclave doesn't rehome orphans, although I could ask my team to ask around if anyone wants a baby. The fact that he's half-vampire and half-werewolf isn't going to make it easy, though."

"What about Fyfe?" Oscar asked.

Ignatius grimaced. "Fyfe doesn't have the patience to deal with babies he can't hand back off to their parents once he's done cuddling them."

"I don't want to hand him off to a stranger, though. With what he is, he could be killed or exploited, and I would never forgive myself for that. I don't think I'd be able to stop worrying about him."

Maria patted Oscar's arm and got up from her chair. "It looks to me like you've made your decision already, Oscar. I hope it works out for you. I'm going to grab some clothes and whatnot from the attic. They'll be old, but clean and functional, and they'll help until you get home and can decide what to do."

Oscar turned to Ignatius as soon as Maria was out of the kitchen where she'd led them when they'd knocked on her door. "I know we haven't talked about anything like this yet."

"You want to keep him." He didn't need to say it for Ignatius to know. Oscar would do the right thing, no matter what it cost him, and keeping this baby and raising him as his own *was* the right thing in this situation. It wasn't what Ignatius had imagined his life with Oscar would be, but there was no changing this. They had to deal with it. They couldn't ignore it, and just like Oscar, Ignatius wouldn't be able to live with himself if he wasn't sure the baby would be safe and loved. He'd seen what could happen to dhampirs over the hundreds of years he'd lived, and he wouldn't wish that on his worse enemies.

"I do." Oscar grimaced. "I can't say I expected to become a dad at twenty-four, not until my father told me he'd arranged a marriage with the daughter of that other pack. But even then, it was nebulous, you know? I knew I'd have to father kids, but this." He looked down at the baby. "This is very real, and yes, I want to keep him. I want to give him the life I didn't have. I want to give him the love he deserves. I do understand why it might mean the end of our relationship, though. I don't expect you to agree to become his second father."

"That's not going to be a problem."

"It's not?"

The baby whimpered, and Ignatius held his hands out. It had been a long while since he'd last taken care of a baby, but he knew what he was doing. "He needs to be changed, and probably to be fed before we leave." Oren had to be wondering where they were, but he hadn't called yet, and Ignatius was glad. He needed a moment to explain what was happening to him.

At least they already had a car seat.

Ignatius guided Oscar through taking out what they needed from the diaper bag, then quickly changed the baby. "You know, we're going to have to choose a name for him," he said as he handed the baby back to Oscar.

"I wanted to be sure he was a boy before we did that." Oscar paused and smiled at the baby. "And that you were on board. I mean, if we're both doing this, if we're doing it together, then we should choose his name together, too. I don't have a name with a special significance for me, but maybe you do?"

Ignatius grinned. "I'm tempted to call him Fyfe, but then the grown-up Fyfe would get a huge head."

Oscar laughed. "Okay, not Fyfe. But maybe he could be Uncle Fyfe? Especially if he's going to let us stay with the coven."

"He is. The baby isn't going to change that. You're a coven member now. They're your family."

"So are you. I know this isn't going to be easy, especially with your job for the conclave."

"We can talk about that later. Right now, we should choose a name, take whatever Maria is going to give us, and go home."

"I'm all for that. What do you want to call our son, then?"

The words *our son* made something tighten in Ignatius' chest. He hadn't planned on this. He hadn't planned on Oscar, on becoming a father, but it felt *right*. He'd thrown himself into his work because he didn't have a personal life. Now he had one, and even though what he did for the conclave was still important to him, it was easy to take a step back from it. "My father's name was Adriano," he said.

"I like it."

"Maybe we can go with the anglicized name? Adrian?"

"Adrian, Oscar, and Ignatius. What do you think?"

"That those are a lot of vowels."

Oscar laughed, and it was finally a truly happy sound. "We'll be the vowels family."

Ignatius reached out and brought Oscar closer. Oscar snuggled against him, the baby between them, and Ignatius' heart settled.

This was nothing like he'd expected or planned, but that didn't mean it was bad. If anything, he loved the thought of becoming a family with Oscar.

Now he just had to find a way to explain it to Oren and Fyfe and see what would happen. Fyfe would probably be over the moon, but Oren might not, since it meant losing one of his team members. It was time for Ignatius to live for himself rather than his job, though.

CHAPTER SEVEN

"I don't think I can do this," Aubrey said, eying Adrian as if the baby might explode in his face.

Oscar shook his head. "He just ate. I changed him. He's going to fall asleep, I promise. I just want to grab a shower without having to worry about him."

Getting used to fatherhood wasn't a walk in the park. Oscar had known kids were demanding, and Adrian wasn't any different. He ate every four hours, slept and pooped a lot, but while all that took a lot of time and left little of it to sleep or do anything else, Oscar was in love. Adrian was a calm baby who only cried when something was wrong. He slept best when he was against Oscar's or Ignatius' chest. He watched the world with wide eyes that were turning brown. He had little to no hair for now, but Ignatius insisted he'd grow some soon. In the meantime, Oscar always made sure to put a hat on him so he didn't get cold.

He wasn't the only one making sure Adrian was always fed, dressed, and clean, either. James and Fyfe loved taking care of him, James more so than Fyfe. But neither of them were available right now, Ignatius was nowhere to be seen, and Oscar *really* needed a shower.

"Please?" he asked Aubrey again. He made sure to slide his lower lip forward and to bat his eyelashes. He thought he looked like an idiot when he did that, but Aubrey was a sucker for a pout.

Aubrey looked at Adrian again. There was panic in his eyes, so Oscar was surprised when he nodded. "Just the time for you to shower."

"I promise."

Oscar had to help Aubrey hold Adrian the right way, and Aubrey still looked uncomfortable once Adrian had settled down, but he didn't try to hand him back, so Oscar rushed out of the room. He knew that if he stayed, Aubrey was going to try to dodge it or ask a dozen questions, but Oscar was pretty ripe, and he needed that shower *yesterday.*

The bedroom he still shared with Ignatius and that now boasted a crib in the corner was empty when Oscar got there. He briefly wondered where Ignatius had disappeared to, but he knew he'd find out sooner or later, and he didn't want to smell like a goat when he did.

Sure enough, Ignatius was there when Oscar came out of the bathroom wearing only a towel and water drops. He'd placed a basket full of tiny laundry on the bed and was struggling to fold it. Oscar watched him from the bathroom door, and it was *adorable.*

He'd never thought of Ignatius in a domestic setting before Adrian had barreled into their lives. He'd been wrapped up in his new feelings for Ignatius, in what he'd hoped was the start of something he'd never had before. And it had been, but now there was Adrian, and sometimes, Oscar felt like he and Ignatius hadn't had the time to find themselves as a couple. They barely had the time to do stuff together, even with the people who volunteered to keep Adrian. Oscar found himself reluctant to hand him over when it came to most people, and he wasn't sure why.

"You're adorable," he said.

Ignatius didn't seem to be surprised at the sound of Oscar's voice. "I'm folding laundry."

"Tiny laundry. Look at how cute that sock is."

Ignatius held it up. Oscar had no idea where Fyfe had found newborn socks with vampire fangs on them, but they were adorable. "They're socks."

"They're cute socks." Oscar stepped closer to Ignatius. "And you're cute, too."

Ignatius arched a brow and put down the sock. Then he grabbed the hamper and put that on the dresser, freeing the bed. "Why, thank you."

"You already knew I thought you were cute," Oscar said. He knew he was terrible at being seductive, but Ignatius didn't seem to mind.

Ignatius smiled. "I did. And I think you're cute, too."

Oscar stepped into Ignatius' arms. "Yeah? Only cute?"

"Okay, maybe more than cute, especially since you're only wearing a towel right now."

"I could be wearing even less."

"That would be nice." Ignatius hooked his fingers into the towel and pulled. The towel dropped to the floor, leaving Oscar exposed.

It made him squirm. He wasn't used to this kind of intimacy with Ignatius yet. He wasn't used to anyone seeing him naked, and it made him self-conscious, even though he knew Ignatius liked what he was seeing.

"Where's Adrian?" Ignatius asked. His voice was rougher than it had been only a few seconds before.

"With Aubrey."

"Aubrey?"

"I told him I needed a shower."

"We're going to have to be quick, then."

"We are." That wasn't going to be a problem. Oscar still went off like a rocket only after what felt like minutes when they had sex. He hoped that wasn't going to last forever, but Ignatius didn't care, and neither did he. They still both had fun, and they both felt good, which was the important part.

Oscar squeaked when Ignatius grabbed both of his hips and hauled him up. He threw him on top of the bed, and by the time Oscar was done bouncing, Ignatius was already half-naked. He finished pushing his jeans down and climbed onto the bed, and Oscar opened his legs and arms for him.

This was where Ignatius belonged, wasn't it? Between Oscar's arms, in his life, in his heart.

Ignatius was fast but thorough as he prepped Oscar, and Oscar kept his gaze on the ceiling, because if standing naked in front of Ignatius had been intimidating, this was even more so. Having Ignatius' fingers in him felt good, though, so good that it was easy to forget the hint of shame and the urge to hide under the sheets of the bed. He still tried to suck his stomach in, but with what Ignatius was doing to him, he needed to breathe, and he ended up forgetting to do that after the second finger pushed into him.

Ignatius climbed up Oscar's front, pressing kisses on his stomach, on his chest, teasing his nipples with his tongue and stopping when they were face to face. "Ready? Because we have to hurry."

"I'm always ready."

Ignatius chuckled as he raised one of Oscar's legs and grabbed the root of his cock with one hand. "Always?"

"For *you*, always."

Oscar wrapped his arms around Ignatius' neck and kissed him. He hissed when Ignatius pushed into him, but he knew the sensation by now. He knew it was going to burn for a bit, then become everything he could want. And it wasn't only the pleasure—he loved feeling connected to Ignatius, feeling like they were one even though it was only for a bit.

Ignatius continued to cover Oscar's face and throat with kisses and small bites as he moved inside him, and Oscar let himself be carried away by what he felt. It was overwhelming yet so good, and he never wanted it to end.

So of course, there was pounding on the door just as he squeezed his eyes shut and came.

"Oscar?" Aubrey sounded panicked.

Oscar opened his eyes wide and looked at Ignatius. He cleared his throat. "Yeah?"

"He pooed!"

Oscar pressed his lips together. He was *not* going to laugh, not when Ignatius had started moving again. "What are you doing?" he asked in a whisper.

"He can change Adrian's diaper."

"We can't continue."

"Why not? You already came." Ignatius licked Oscar's throat, and Oscar's cock twitched. Oscar groaned.

"Oscar!" Aubrey bellowed.

"Give me the time to dress!"

Oscar couldn't speak after that, because Ignatius was moving inside him, making him feel like he could come again. He didn't—he didn't even get entirely hard again—but the sensations were so *much*. Oscar didn't know what to focus on, so he focused on Ignatius.

"What the fuck, Oscar?" Aubrey yelled. He made a retching sound. "Come on. I *know* Ignatius is in there with you. Did you really lie to me so you could have a quickie? Your son stinks. I think he managed to get poo on the back of his head, and I'm *not* cleaning that."

Oscar buried his face against Ignatius' neck and laughed.

This was his life now. His messy, complicated, beautiful life. He wouldn't have it if he'd left his father when he'd wanted to all those years ago, so maybe being a coward hadn't been such a bad thing after all.

He wouldn't have all this if he'd stood up to his father. Now that he was free, he had a family, and a man who loved him. His life wasn't perfect by any means, but it was as perfect as it could be, and that was more than enough for him.

Pryderi
Catherine Lievens

Excerpt

Nate could only stare at Pryderi. He could tell that wasn't the reaction Pryderi wanted, but he couldn't even think, let alone say anything. "What?" he finally croaked.

Pryderi straightened his back. "You're my mate. I should have told you sooner, but . . ."

"That can't be true. Who put you up to this? Justin? Hunter?" It would be a cruel joke, but people were cruel sometimes, even if they didn't mean to be.

Pryderi's face twisted. "I know I'm not perfect, far from it, and I might not be the person you want to spend the rest of your life with, but I'm not lying."

Shit. He really wasn't, wasn't he? Not that Nate had actually thought he was. He'd half hoped so, because he didn't know how to deal with this. He didn't know how to deal with a mate. He didn't want a mate.

He rubbed his face. "When did you find out?"

"The first time I walked in here. Nix know from sight."

"It's been a while."

Pryderi shrugged, feigning indifference, but Nate could see in his eyes how important this was for him. And why wouldn't it be? He was a Nix, and just like shifters, mates were everything to them. Nate had never seen Pryderi with another man who wasn't his friend, so he didn't think he dated. Even before telling him they were mates, he'd been faithful to him, and wasn't that a hit to the heart?

And that kiss. Pryderi had been hesitant and quick, but Nate doubted he would ever forget the first touch of their lips. He'd been stunned, because he hadn't expected it—and because he'd wanted it much more than he'd been ready to admit to himself. At least now that made sense. He wanted Pryderi because there was a bond between them, even though they weren't mated yet.

Nate couldn't think about mating right now, not when his brain was sending him vastly different outputs. He wanted to pull Pryderi into his arms and drag him upstairs to his apartment, but he needed to keep him at arm's length. He didn't want to hurt Pryderi, and that was what an outright rejection would do, but he also didn't want to give Pryderi false hope.

Nate sighed and leaned against the counter. "You're sure?" he asked.

"Of course I am."

"Of course you are." Nate had no idea how to deal with this. "You're younger than me."

Pryderi's jaw tightened. "I am. I'm twenty-one."

He was so painfully young. Nate didn't want to hurt him, but he couldn't ruin that youth and the hope that went along with it.

He didn't want to make Pryderi sad. He didn't want to hurt him. He knew that was most likely because of the bond, but that didn't change anything. "I don't know what to say."

"You don't have to say anything. I realize how huge this can feel. When I first saw you and knew you were my mate, I didn't know what to do. I didn't tell anyone, because it felt like I should tell you first, but I could have used someone to talk to."

"I'm sorry you felt like you couldn't, and like you couldn't tell me right away."

"I should have, but I was afraid, I suppose."

Of rejection? He'd read Nate right, if that was the case. "You're too young to want to be with me."

Pryderi's eyes narrowed. "I think I should be the one to decide that, shouldn't I?"

"Of course, but—"

"You're saying I shouldn't want to be with you because you're old."

That was a hit to the heart. "I guess I am. I'm forty-two, and while I know you're going to live to be more than a hundred, you're not that old now. You're young. You're an enforcer. I'm old, and I have a bad back." Nate honestly didn't see why Pryderi would want to be with him. He probably wouldn't if it weren't for the mate bond, and he couldn't help but wonder what deity Pryderi had pissed off to get saddled with a mate like him.

These were the moments in which Nate wished he could call his brother and ask him for advice. Cal would have known what to say to Pryderi to reject him without hurting him, but Nate had no idea where to start. The fact that his heart was rebelling against not having Pryderi in his life didn't help. In his head, he knew it would be the best thing for Pryderi, but he couldn't deny he wanted what Pryderi was offering.

He wanted the companionship. He wanted someone waiting for him at home when he was done working, warming his bed, his heart, and his life. Owning a bar wasn't the perfect job by far. Some months, it was hard to pay all the bills. The hours were shit, and Nate had to deal with rude customers and smile at them even though he wanted nothing more than to punch them. And of course, there was his back. He'd been dealing with the pain since the car accident, and he was used to it. He hated it, but it was just one more thing he had to live with.

But Pryderi didn't. He didn't have to do anything, even though he seemed set on wiggling his way into Nate's life. Nate should tell him *no*. He should tell him he didn't want anything from him, that he didn't want a mate, but he'd be lying if he did that. He wanted everything Pryderi was offering.

He still couldn't accept it.

Even if he could get over the age difference and the fact that Pryderi was little more than a teenager, there was still Pryderi's job to deal with, and Nate wasn't sure he could. He'd already lost the most important person in his life. It had taken him years to get over his brother's disappearance, and some days, he realized he was still hurting over it. He probably always would. What would happen if he said yes to Pryderi and he lost him to his job, though?

That was a heartbreak Nate didn't want to think about.

Pryderi sighed. "I know you're not exactly happy about this. I can see it on your face. But please, give me a chance. We can be friends and see where things go from there."

"It would be better not to."

Pryderi glared. Nate had thought he was shy and meek, but he could see the spine of steel that made him a good enforcer now. "Why not? Because you think you're old?"

"I am."

"You're older than me, sure. That doesn't mean anything, though."

"I'm hurt. I have a bad back."

"And a few of my fingers hurt when it rains because I broke them when I was a kid. So what if your back hurts? It doesn't make you less of a man."

Nate wasn't ready to tell Pryderi about Cal. He wasn't sure he ever would, although from the way Pryderi was pushing, Nate could too easily imagine how he'd bury his way under his skin. Nate would fall in love with him if he gave himself the chance to. "I know it doesn't."

"But you still think I should stay away, that I can get better." Pryderi leaned closer.

He smelled of violet, which wasn't a scent Nate usually associated with men, but he would from now on.

"I can't get better. You're my mate. That means you're the perfect man for me, no matter how cheesy that sounds. So before pushing me away and deciding for me that I'm better off without you, think about that. Think about what you'd take from me if you did that."

"Pryderi—"

"No. You're my one chance at this, Nate."

"You can find love without needing it to be with your mate. With me."

"I can. I don't want to. I want you, and nothing you can say will change my mind. You can decide you don't want me, and that's okay. But don't hide behind the thought that you're doing it for me. You're not. I'm the one who gets to decide that, not you. So if you don't want me, be honest. That's all I'm asking for."

It was, but Nate could see the pain in Pryderi's eyes, the unshed tears that were already making them glint in the bars' light.

He couldn't do it. He couldn't hurt Pryderi, not right now. "Why don't you give me your phone number?" he said instead of what he ought to say.

About the Author

Catherine lives in Italy, country of good food and hot men. She used to write fantasy as a child, but it was reading her first gay erotic romance novel that made her realize that that was what she really wanted to write.

After graduating from college in English language and translation, she divides her day between writing, reading, taking care of her son and reading some more.

You can find her on Facebook and Twitter or on her website: authorcatherinelievens.wordpress.com

Email: lievens.catherine@gmail.com

Newsletter: http://eepurl.com/c-uvKn

www.ingramcontent.com/pod-product-compliance
Lightning Source LLC
Chambersburg PA
CBHW060635130626
46555CB00002B/811